Longarm tri[...] cheap lock fo[...] opened the sturdy main blade. He slipped that between the door and the frame and made contact with the lock bar.

Pressing forward to give the tip of the blade some purchase on the cheap steel of the lock, he prised the bar sideways until it cleared the mortise. The door swung open easily after that.

The room inside was dark but the moaning continued to come from it. Longarm reached into his vest pocket for a match and snapped it aflame with his thumbnail.

He strode forward, found a lamp in the middle of a small table, and lit it. Lamplight flooded the tiny room to disclose Will Carver, his face a pulped mass of blood, lying on the floor in front of the fireplace.

DON'T MISS THESE
ALL-ACTION WESTERN SERIES
FROM THE BERKLEY PUBLISHING GROUP

THE GUNSMITH by J. R. Roberts
Clint Adams was a legend among lawmen, outlaws, and ladies.
They called him . . . the Gunsmith.

LONGARM by Tabor Evans
The popular long-running series about Deputy U.S. Marshal
Custis Long—his life, his loves, his fight for justice.

SLOCUM by Jake Logan
Today's longest-running action Western. John Slocum rides a
deadly trail of hot blood and cold steel.

BUSHWHACKERS by B. J. Lanagan
An action-packed series by the creators of Longarm! The rous-
ing adventures of the most brutal gang of cutthroats ever
assembled—Quantrill's Raiders.

DIAMONDBACK by Guy Brewer
Dex Yancey is Diamondback, a Southern gentleman turned
con man when his brother cheats him out of the family fortune.
Ladies love him. Gamblers hate him. But nobody pulls one
over on Dex . . .

WILDGUN by Jack Hanson
The blazing adventures of mountain man Will Barlow—from
the creators of Longarm!

TEXAS TRACKER by Tom Calhoun
J.T. Law: the most relentless—and dangerous—manhunter in
all Texas. Where sheriffs and posses fail, he's the best man to
bring in the most vicious outlaws—for a price.

TABOR EVANS

LONGARM

AND THE
STAGECOACH ROBBERS

J
JOVE BOOKS, NEW YORK

BERKLEY PUBLISHING GROUP
Published by the Penguin Group
Penguin Group (USA) LLC
375 Hudson Street, New York, New York 10014

USA • Canada • UK • Ireland • Australia • New Zealand • India • South Africa • China

penguin.com

A Penguin Random House Company

LONGARM AND THE STAGECOACH ROBBERS

A Jove Book / published by arrangement with the author

For information, address: The Berkley Publishing Group,
a division of Penguin Group (USA) LLC,
375 Hudson Street, New York, New York 10014.

ISBN: 978-0-515-15487-0

PUBLISHING HISTORY
Jove mass-market edition / December 2014

PRINTED IN THE UNITED STATES OF AMERICA

10 9 8 7 6 5 4 3 2 1

Cover illustration by Milo Sinovcic.

Chapter 1

United States Marshal William Vail looked up from the telegram on his desk, a scowl flickering across his normally bland expression. He peered at his deputy and said, "I have some work for you, Long."

"Not more warrants t' serve, I hope," Deputy Marshal Custis Long said.

"No, Longarm, I just got this. It's a gang that has been robbing the mail. They've hit the Carver Express Company twice in the past month, and the local law isn't doing anything to stop them. At least not according to what the express line people believe. That could just be a matter of personal differences. I wouldn't venture an opinion about that. But there is no question that robbery of the mail falls under our jurisdiction as a Federal crime. I want you to go look into it."

"Carver," Longarm repeated. Then he shook his head. "Don't think I'm familiar with that line, boss."

"Yes, you are, just not by that name. Carver bought out Henry Blaisdell up in South Park. You knew Henry. This is the same deal under a different name. But they took over Henry's mail contract along with everything else," Vail said.

"Ah, them I know," Longarm conceded. "Two robberies of the mail?" he asked.

The balding but still lethal U.S. marshal nodded. "Yes, and that makes it our business, not just Carver's."

Longarm nodded. A tall man with seal brown hair and a sweeping handlebar mustache, he was a study in brown and black. The deputy wore a brown tweed coat, a calfskin vest, and brown corduroy trousers tucked into black stovepipe boots. Perhaps more important, he also wore a black gun belt strapped around narrow hips, the holster carried on his belly canted for a cross-draw and containing a double-action Colt .45 revolver.

He reached into his coat for a cheroot, bit the twist off, and spat the bit of tobacco into his palm but, seeing Billy Vail's scowl, did not light the slender cigar.

"I'll grab my bag an' catch the next train up to Fairplay," he said.

Vail nodded. "Henry has the schedule," he said, the Henry this time referring to his clerk.

Fairplay was the major mining community in the South Park area. The railroad had recently reached it. The rest of the surrounding area of South Park was served by the stagecoach line formerly owned by Blaisdell and now, apparently, by Carver. Under either ownership, the mail contract gave the government a certain amount of authority and privilege.

"If you find that you need help," Vail said, "it's as close as the telegraph line. Keep that in mind."

Deputy Custis Long nodded. "Don't I always."

"As a matter of fact, no, you don't always," Vail said. "But do keep it in mind this time."

"Whatever you say, boss," Longarm told him. The tone of his voice suggested that he did not at all mean it. But the prudent thing was to say it anyway.

Longarm touched his forehead with one finger in salute, then left Billy Vail's office. He retrieved his flat-crowned, snuff brown Stetson from the hat rack in the outer office and stopped at Henry's desk to collect a fistful of expense vouchers before he headed home to get his carpetbag.

Chapter 2

"There won't be another passenger coach up-bound until tomorrow," the helpful clerk told him, "but if you hurry, you can catch the ore cars going to Fairplay. The only passenger leaving this evening is going to Silver Plume and that isn't even the right direction. You want the Como route. But if you want to catch that one, you'll need to hurry."

"Do I have time to get my bag?" Longarm asked.

"If you rush, you should make it."

Longarm hurried out of the stately Federal Building on Denver's Colfax Avenue and hailed a cab. He climbed onto the metal step at the side of the passenger compartment and gave the address of his boardinghouse.

"And hurry. There's something extra in it for you if you get me to my train on time."

"You got it, gov'nor," the hack driver said.

The man applied his whip and got Longarm home in record time.

"Wait here. I need to grab my bag and be right back."

"Say, I've heard that one before. Once you're gone,

mister, I won't ever see you again," the cabbie said with a grunt of disgust.

"Shit, if you don't think I'm telling you the truth, mister, climb down from there and come with me," Longarm suggested.

The driver took him up on it, stepping down from his driving box and clipping a weight to his horse's bit. "All right, now where?" he said.

The man followed Longarm into the boardinghouse and upstairs to Longarm's room. His carpetbag was always kept packed and ready for travel so it was only a matter of moments to grab it, take a last look around to make sure he was not forgetting anything—although he probably was— and head back downstairs.

"All right. You wasn't lying to me," the cabbie admitted. He seemed almost disappointed to discover that his fare had been honest about his intentions. "Now where?"

"Train station," Longarm said.

"Which one?"

"Fairplay."

"I'll have you there in jig time, mister," the cabbie promised as he unfastened the horse from its tether and mounted the driving box. Longarm entered the cab, and the driver took up his lines and cracked his whip over the horse's ears.

True to his word, the man delivered Longarm to the train depot just in time for him to catch the up-bound string of now empty ore cars. They would load through the night and bring mineral-bearing ores back down to the Denver smelters the next day.

There was no passenger accommodation, but as a deputy United States marshal, Longarm was entitled to passage amid the smoke and cinders in the caboose.

Longarm handed a generous tip to the cab driver, picked up his carpetbag, and headed for the depot.

Chapter 3

It was nearly midnight when Longarm stepped down onto the cinders near the loading chutes in Fairplay, Colorado. The train crew would work through the night loading ore from the several mines in and near the small town and carry the ore down to Denver the next day.

In the meantime Longarm needed to find accommodations for his stay in the South Park area, where the mail thefts were occurring.

He hefted his carpetbag, took a last puff on the cheroot he had been smoking, and tossed the butt onto the tracks.

The town was large enough to have two good hotels, another not so good, and a number of cheap flophouses where the hardrock miners slept. Longarm headed for the Pickens House. He had stayed there before.

"Marshal Long!" the desk clerk greeted him when he entered the lobby. The man sounded genuinely pleased to see him.

It took Longarm a moment to call the man's name to mind. "Hello, Nathan. Would you have a room for me? I may be here for a few days."

"Please, Marshal." Nathan sounded offended. "We always have a place for you."

Nathan rang a small bell and moments later a sleepy-eyed bellhop came groggily out of a back room. "Yes, sir?"

"Take Marshal Long's bag up to room eight, Johnny."

"Yes, sir." The boy came around the registration desk to take Longarm's carpetbag and lead the way upstairs to the small but clean and tidy room.

"Would you like a pitcher of water, sir?"

Longarm nodded and the kid, awake now, hurried away. Longarm did not know how far the boy had to go to fetch the water, but he was back almost immediately carrying a full pitcher.

"Do you want a tub or anything?" the kid asked.

"No, this will do for tonight." Longarm gave the boy a nickel and bolted the door behind him.

He stripped to his drawers and gave himself a quick wash to get rid of the feel of smoke and cinders left by riding at the back of the ore train then crawled gratefully into the clean sheets of the Pickens House's bed.

He still had the sense that he could almost feel the rumbling vibrations of the train and the monotonous click of the rails, but that did not stop him from dropping off to sleep within seconds of lying down.

Chapter 4

Longarm slept until well past dawn, unusual for him, but woke up refreshed. He dressed quickly and went downstairs to an overpriced breakfast—fifty cents for flapjacks and porridge, with no meat included. So much for the hotel dining room, at least in the morning.

From there he walked through town until he found a barber shop and joined a small group of men waiting for shaves. Longarm kept his mouth closed and ears open, but no one was talking about the robberies. The barber, however, gave him a good shave and a splash of bay rum.

"Any idea where I can find the stage line office?" Longarm asked when he got out of the chair.

"Mister, you have to be new in Fairplay. There isn't so much of it that anything could be hard to find. You just go down to the end of this block and turn right. The stagecoach depot is at the end of that block on your left."

Longarm nodded and paid the man for his shave. "Thanks. Reckon I'll see you again now an' then."

"Any time. I'm here every day but Sundays," the barber said, turning and beckoning for the next man in line.

Longarm exited the barber shop and ambled down the street and around the corner. Ahead he could see a set of corrals with heavy-bodied horses standing there swishing their tails. When he got closer, he could see the sign painted onto the tall false front over the building porch: CARVER EXPRESS CO., DAILY SCHEDULES, CHARLIE CARVER, PROP.

He paused outside long enough to light a cheroot, then entered the stagecoach line office. There was a blond, middle-aged woman behind the counter fussing with some paperwork. She looked up when Longarm came in, a tiny bell over the door tinkling to announce his arrival.

"Can I help you, sir? Our coach has already left on today's run, but there will be another tomorrow."

Longarm leaned on the counter and produced his badge. "I'm hoping that I can help you folks, ma'am." He introduced himself and said, "I'd like t' speak with Mr. Carver if I may."

The woman laughed. It was an old joke for her. "I am Charlie Carver, Marshal, Charlie being short for Charlise. And yes, you may certainly speak with me. What can I do for you?"

"You can tell me the lay o' things here. All I know is that there's been some robberies o' the mail. That and the fact that Fairplay is serviced by the railroad now but you still have stagecoach service. So tell me about it, please."

"Would you like to come back to my office, Marshal? I have some fresh coffee on the stove there."

"Coffee sounds just fine, ma'am," he said, removing his hat.

She unlatched the flimsy gate that separated the lobby area from the ticket desk and motioned him inside. Her private office lay behind the ticket section. There seemed to be no other employees present. But then she had said that the Carver coach had already rolled for the day's run.

"Sit down, please. Can you take your coffee black? I don't keep any condiments. I never use them myself."

"Black would be fine."

Charlie poured two cups and handed one to Longarm before she sat at her rolltop desk and turned her swivel chair around to face him. "What do you need to know, Marshal?"

"How's about we start with everything an' go from there?" Longarm said.

"Before we get into this, would you mind putting that cigar out? I'm allergic to them."

"Yes, ma'am." Longarm crossed his legs and dutifully stubbed his ash out on the sole of his boot. He looked around, but there were no ashtrays or spittoons in the room so he tucked the cold cheroot into his pocket. "Now, where were we?"

Chapter 5

He liked the woman's way of speaking. Calm, clear, and matter of fact.

While Longarm listened, he sat looking at Charlie Carver. He liked what he saw. She was a handsome female although she tried not to show it. He guessed she wanted to be judged for what she did rather than what she looked like. That was a reasonable enough attitude. But she was a damned good-looking woman nonetheless.

"There have been three robberies," she said.

"Three? I thought there were only the two."

"Then you didn't hear about the one yesterday evening."

"No, I didn't."

"It was the same as the other two," Charlie said. "This is a small operation. We have only the one coach, and I don't employ a shotgun guard to ride along. There hasn't been any reason to worry about robbers expecting to take a gold shipment. Hasn't been ever since the railroad reached Fairplay, and the trains began carrying ores down to Denver for smelting."

"What did they do before that?" Longarm asked.

"They processed the ore up here as best they could, but everyone concedes that they were only able to extract a small percentage of the metal that way. Down below in the big smelters they achieve almost a ninety percent extraction.

"The point is, of course, that we simply don't carry anything of great value on our little route," she said.

"Tell me about the route," Longarm said.

Charlie shrugged. "There isn't that much to it. We run six days a week. Not on Sundays. Mondays, Wednesdays, and Fridays we make a circle in one direction. Tuesdays, Thursdays, and Saturdays we turn around and make the same circle but in the opposite direction.

"We service Bailey, Lake George, Guffey, and Hartsel. It's just a big circle. We carry passengers, a little freight, and of course, the mail pouches. The Hedley brothers have a line that runs from Colorado Springs up through South Park and down through Trout Creek Pass to the Arkansas River Valley and on to Leadville. Our lines intersect at Hartsel. I don't know if you are familiar with the hotel and the baths there.

"Anyway, we exchange mail pouches at the hotel in Hartsel. Anything coming on to Fairplay we take. Anything to be carried down to Manitou or Colorado City or the like we send down by way of the Hedleys.

"To tell you the truth, Marshal, our little line depends on the income we receive for carrying those mail pouches. There is precious little regular income beyond that. There are very few passengers nowadays and even less freight, so it comes down to the mail. What I fear is that our mail contract will be revoked if we can't deliver."

The woman stood and began to pace and clench her hands together.

"Ours is a tiny line. Even smaller since the railroad got

here and our service area was reduced. Now it is just my driver and me. He takes care of the horses and the driving. I take care of the office."

Longarm reached for a cheroot by habit, remembered the lady's allergy, and took his hand away. "How'd you come to own the line?" he asked.

"I am a widow, Marshal. Bertram and I were married for more than twenty years. He was a mining engineer. He was killed in an accident underground. The company paid me a small death benefit plus Bert had taken out a life insurance policy. Between them, I would have had enough to live on for a few years, but then my funds would have been exhausted. I needed to find a source of income. I knew Hank Blaisdell was thinking of selling out and retiring to California, so I made him an offer. This is the result."

Longarm nodded. "An' if the line folds?" he asked.

"I really don't know. I have no skills." She laughed, a sound with no mirth in it whatsoever. "I'm even too old to become a prostitute. I don't know what I could possibly do to survive without this little express line."

Longarm smiled. "Then let's us see what we can do t' keep any o' that from happening, shall we? An' the first thing we need t' do is to find whoever it is that's been robbing your coach an' put 'em behind bars. I'll need to talk with your driver. When will he get back?"

"He won't be back until evening, but of course I will introduce you to him," she said.

"All right, thanks."

"Is there anything else I can tell you? Anything I can do?"

"Not right now," he said, "but if I think of anything, I'll let y' know."

"Anything," she said. "Anything at all."

Longarm stood and thanked her again then stepped outside. He was wanting a smoke in the worst way.

But then he probably would not have been thinking so much about smoking except for the fact that he was not able to. That made him want a cheroot all the more. And as soon as he was out the door to the street, he was reaching into his pocket for that cigar he had not been able to finish inside.

Chapter 6

The beer at Ikey Tyler's Bearpaw Saloon was flat and the whores ugly, but the beer cost only a nickel a mug—Longarm had no idea what the whores cost and was not interested in finding out—and the place had a good flow of customers even at the morning hour.

That would be because several of the mines in the district operated around the clock, and because the shifts worked on varying hours, it was evening for someone nearly all the time.

Longarm parked himself in the center of Tyler's bar and nursed his beer. Not many people in Fairplay knew him as a Federal marshal. Not yet. He wanted to take advantage of that time to eavesdrop on the conversations around him for as long as he could.

He was hoping to hear some talk about the robberies. What he got was mostly bellyaching about the work underground—the poor quality of the tools, the scarcity of the rest breaks, and stupidity of the bosses—but also a fair amount of bragging. The braggadocio mostly involved the whores. To hear the men tell it about themselves, they were

so big the whores would take one look and turn them down
or they were such good lovers that the girls would refuse
payment for the privilege of being fucked.

Longarm had to hide a smile behind the rim of his mug
when he heard those boasts. A man who had to brag on how
good he was probably wasn't.

There was a fair amount of talk about a prizefight that
was scheduled for the weekend. A promoter from Buena
Vista down in the Arkansas River valley was in town hawk-
ing his fighter against any comers. Five dollars to get in the
ring with the man and a hundred back to anyone who could
last five minutes without leaving his feet.

That was the sort of contest that would draw crowds from
the whole South Park area, Longarm knew. Hell, if he hadn't
been here on duty, it was something he might take a chance
on himself.

As it was, it was a contest he intended to observe. He was
willing to bet that the stagecoach robbers would attend. Not
that he would know who they were. Not at the time. Hope-
fully he would get some clue as to who and where.

If nothing else, he always enjoyed a good prizefight.

"Another beer, mister?"

Longarm looked up, his concentration broken. "Uh, no,
I'm good here."

"Mister, this here is a place for folks who want to have
a drink. You understand? Now either drink or get the fuck
out of here. I don't need any help to prop up the bar. Get it?"

"I'll have another," Longarm said, digging a nickel out
of his pocket and laying it on the bar.

Chapter 7

Longarm had lunch at a pleasant café he remembered from past visits. It lay on the east side of town, close to the creek that was the headwaters of the South Platte River . . . although it did not look anything like an important waterway at its beginning. What it did look like was a nice little brook where a man might find a trout or two. Longarm regretted leaving his rod and selection of flies at home. But perhaps if he found time . . .

He took his time over lunch and gave thought to whether he could get away with pretending to be someone up here for the prizefight. Or to go fishing.

Reluctantly he gave up that idea. Too many people in Fairplay knew him to be a deputy U.S. marshal.

That seemed a pity, though. He would have especially enjoyed acting the part of a fisherman on holiday.

As it was, he finished his slab of elk steak and fried spuds, paid for the meal and left a modest tip, then walked across town to the tall, imposing Park County Courthouse, which overlooked the west outskirts of Fairplay.

He climbed to the third floor, where the sheriff had his office and jail.

"Afternoon, Marshal. What can we do for you?" the on-duty deputy asked when Longarm walked in.

"Is Bud in?"

"Sorry, Marshal. The sheriff is down in El Paso County attending a conference. Is there anything I can do for you?"

Longarm approached the desk to shake hands. "Please forgive me, but I've forgotten your name."

"Chance Hardesty," the deputy said.

"Can you tell me anything about these stagecoach robberies, Chance?"

"Is that what brings you up here?" Hardesty leaned back in his chair and shook his head. "I wish I had something to tell you, but if I knew anything, I'd have someone in the jail back there." He hooked a thumb over his shoulder.

"I have to admit," he said, "that with the sheriff gone, I've been too busy to do anything but take down a report about them. There's a prizefight scheduled for this weekend."

"I heard something 'bout that," Longarm said.

"Right. Well, it's drawing a lot of low types up here. Pickpockets and confidence artists, that sort of trash. Me and Tom . . . do you remember him? Him and me are all the law there is in the county right now, and the sheriff wants one of us behind this desk here at all times to take any complaints and see to the jail, like that. Tom is out somewhere right now trying to keep an eye on things, and today I'm the one stuck in here. Tomorrow it will be his turn to sit and be bored."

Longarm remembered Park County Deputy Tom Bitterman as a happy-go-lucky kid who was more interested in getting free rolls in the hay from the local whores than he was in performing his duties. But then Tommy was Sheriff Bud Jahn's nephew or some such kin and was secure in his position no matter how poorly he performed.

Maybe, Longarm thought, he was being too harsh in his assessment. Maybe Tommy had grown up some since the last time Longarm was up here.

"Can I take a look at those reports you wrote out?" Longarm asked.

"Sure thing, Marshal." Hardesty jumped up and crossed the room to a tall file cabinet. He pulled out a drawer, riffled through the file folders there, found the one he wanted, and pulled it out.

"All three of them are in here," he said, handing the folder to Longarm. "Would you like to use the desk here to sit and go over them?" He smiled and added, "I'd like to go down and take a shit anyway, and that way there'd still be someone behind the desk. Would you mind?"

"Go ahead," Longarm said. "I won't let anybody swipe the jail while you're away."

"Thanks. I was afraid I was going to have to use the thunder mug, and then I'd just have to clean it out later." Hardesty grabbed his hat and was headed down the stairs before Longarm had a chance to change his mind.

Chapter 8

Longarm was disappointed. It was not that he had really expected to learn anything new or illuminating from the Park County sheriff's incidence reports. But he had certainly hoped.

As it was, reading through the reports told him nothing more than Charlise Carver already had. In each instance the coach was stopped by two men—well, at least two; there could have been someone else hiding nearby—who held shotguns. One threatened the horses; the other targeted the driver. Neither man spoke.

Longarm sat back in the sheriff's swivel chair and scratched under his chin. He was making an assumption to think that the robbers were men. They wore dusters that hung from head to toe plus slouch hats and bandannas. One or both could as easily have been women. It was something to keep in mind.

He leaned forward and concentrated on the reports, and again all three were similar. The robbers did not speak. They merely motioned with the barrels of their shotguns.

The driver threw the mail pouches down, along with any

other express messages, then the robbers stepped back and
motioned for the coach to proceed. Which it did, just as fast
as it could go.

Longarm did not at all fault the driver. He was not armed
and had the lives of his passengers to consider.

Which brought something else to mind.

Longarm shuffled through the incidence reports again.
On one trip the coach was empty. On another there was one
passenger, and on the third there were three passengers. On
no occasion did the robbers attempt to hold up the passengers. They were completely ignored even though it would
have been simple enough for the robbers to strip them of
cash or valuables while the coach was stopped.

That was not at all an ordinary way for a stagecoach rob-
ber to act.

They took only the mail pouches. Those pouches, empty,
were found lying beside the road on the next trip around.

That, too, seemed odd.

Longarm took out a cheroot and lit it—at least here he
could smoke while he pondered—then laced his hands
behind his head and thought about the reports he had in
front of him.

They told him little. All three robberies occurred on the
Bailey to Lake George leg of the run. All southbound, that
is, from Bailey down to Lake George and not from Lake
George back north to Bailey on the other side of that run.

Perhaps someone in Bailey was expected to mail something that the robbers wanted to intercept? The conjecture
was thin but certainly possible.

Longarm sat smoking—and thinking—until Deputy
Hardesty returned from taking his overdue shit.

"Feel better?" Longarm asked with a smile.

"Lots. Thanks."

"Glad t' do it for a fellow badge carrier." Longarm stood,

stretched, and turned the chair back over to Chance Hardesty. "If I think of anything else, I might be back," he said.

"Any time at all, Marshal. The sheriff is always glad to help."

Longarm touched the brim of his Stetson and headed back down the steep stairs.

Chapter 9

He idled the afternoon away, wandering from one to another of Fairplay's many saloons, nursing a beer in each and keeping his ears open. The effort was wasted. Well, except for discovering which of the slop joints had the best beer or the prettiest whores. He learned a bit about that; unfortunately, that was not what he was interested in.

When he heard the Carver stagecoach rattle in, the jehu cracking his whip and making a show of the arrival, Longarm shoved his beer mug away and went out to greet the coach.

The driver surprised him. The fellow looked like he was barely old enough to shave. Hell, maybe he didn't. He knew how to handle the whip and the driving lines, though. He brought the lathered four-up in with a swirl of dust and a high-pitched yip.

Charlise Carver came out of the office to greet him.

Charlise, Longarm thought. Now why had he taken to thinking of her as Charlise instead of as Charlie?

He took another look at the woman, standing in the afternoon sun, and realized what the difference was. Of a sudden he was thinking about her as a damned attractive woman and not just a victim of crime.

Not that she had given him any reason to think that way. But he did.

The driver set the brake and Charlise opened the coach door. There were two passengers. They climbed down, brushing at their clothing and chatting back and forth.

The passengers retrieved their bags from the boot at the back of the coach, Charlise standing with them, thanking them for their business and expressing the usual platitudes about hoping they had a good trip.

Meanwhile the driver climbed down off the rig. He, too, brushed the dust from his linen duster—well named—and removed his heavy gloves.

"Will," Charlise said, beckoning him over to where Longarm stood. "I want you to meet U.S. Marshal Long." She looked at Longarm and raised an eyebrow. "Curtis, is it?"

"Custis," he corrected.

"Custis, meet my son and business partner, Will C. Carver."

The young man grinned and stuck a hand out to shake. "My pleasure, Marshal."

"Only a deputy," Longarm said. "The marshal is down in Denver settin' behind a desk while I'm up here tryin' to find out what's up with these robberies. Did you have any trouble today?"

"No, sir. It was all smooth. Took one fella from Bailey down to Lake George, picked up those two in Hartsel, and brought them over here."

"You were carrying mail today?" Longarm asked.

"Yes, sir. Every day. Two pouches from Bailey, one coming here and the other going down to Buena Vista and beyond. One pouch from Colorado City and Manitou coming here."

As if to affirm that, the postmaster showed up to collect the pair of canvas pouches.

"Do you two know each other?" Charlise asked.

Both men shook their heads.

"Deputy Marshal Long, this is our postmaster, Jon Willoughby. Jon, this gentleman is Custis Long. He came up from Denver to look into these mail robberies."

They shook and Willoughby said, "I hope you can clear this up, Deputy. We can't have such a thing. No, sir, not at all."

Willboughby was a small man with thinning gray hair. He seemed fussy and nervous, perhaps prissy. Almost certainly a political appointee. Which meant that as a Federal employee whose bosses for the most part were politicians of one stripe or another, Custis Long should watch his step around Postmaster Willoughby.

"Excuse me, please," Longarm said, nodding and touching the brim of his Stetson. He walked over to the front of the coach, where Will Carver had retired. "Help you with these horses?" he offered.

"I can handle them."

"Sure you can, but I'd like to help."

"All right, thanks. We'll take them around back still in harness then pull the harness and rub each down before turning it loose in the corrals. Then once they're fed and settled, I'll clean the harness and lay it out ready for tomorrow."

"Different team tomorrow?" Longarm asked.

"Oh, yes, of course. We use three teams plus a pair of fill-ins for if one gets sick or is lamed. We change the team in Lake George, so the horses only go in one direction when we take them out. Then they get to rest until it's their turn to come back, either the next day or the day after."

"Well, let's us get these boys cleaned up and fed an' settled in for the night," Longarm said, taking the bit chain of the near leader.

Chapter 10

There was a small barn behind the express company office. Will and Longarm led the heavy cobs inside and tied them to rings set high on the support posts then groomed them and cared for their feet before leading them out to one of the small corrals, where they had a good supply of mixed grass and alfalfa hay in a bunk.

Will Carver pumped the trough nearly full with clean water, wiped his hands, and with a grin said, "Thanks, Marshal. That was good of you to help."

"Glad t' do it, kid. Say, you handle these big boys just fine."

"Them and me get along good." He laughed. "When I was a button, I was all the time sneaking out of school so I could fool around with Mr. Blaisdell's horses." The laugh turned into a grin. "And now they're our horses, Mom and me. They know me real well."

"I expect they do. Coffee? Or a drink?" Longarm asked.

"I could use a cup of coffee. Mom doesn't like for me to drink it, but I've liked that since I was a button, too."

"Then let's go over to the café and get a couple cups. I

want t' ask you about the robberies. Everything you can remember 'bout them an' then I'll pump you for stuff you don't even know that you know."

"Whatever you want. We need to stop these robberies. I don't suppose it's any secret that we're riding right on the edge. If we lose our mail contract, we're fucked."

From the way the young fellow said that, Longarm suspected he did not want his mother to know he used language like that. Still, Longarm could not blame him. Their whole livelihood depended on the express company. And the express company depended on the mail contract.

"How much money is involved here?" Longarm asked as they walked down the dusty street toward a small café on the corner.

"Sixty-five dollars a month," Will said. He shrugged and added, "The contract amount was set before the railroad got up this far. There was a lot more mail to carry then. You, uh, you won't say anything about that, will you?"

"Mail isn't my department so I got no cause t' stick my nose in there. All I care about is the law. An' the law says folks aren't supposed to fuck with the United States mail." He clapped the young man on the shoulder and said, "An' that *is* my department."

"Good. Then can you catch the sons of bitches quick, please?"

Longarm chuckled and led the way into the café, where pie and coffee waited.

Chapter 11

"I'd better go now," Will said an hour or so later. "Mom will be expecting me for dinner. Uh, Marshal, don't tell her I had anything to eat, will you, please?"

"Sure, no problem," Longarm told him.

Will Carver excused himself from the table, thanked Longarm, and left. Longarm remained in the café and had supper, then in the early evening ambled over to the nearest saloon for a drink.

The whiskey spread its warmth through his belly.

"Another?" the barman offered.

Longarm nodded. The first had been good. The second was even better. He turned with his back to the bar and contemplated the gaming tables. He thoroughly enjoyed the game of poker although he did not claim to be an expert at the play. His purpose was relaxation when he played, not income.

At the moment the few tables in the place were already occupied. If a seat came open, he would consider asking in, but there would be time enough to think about that if or when it happened. In the meantime he intended to relax. The thought of another whiskey was pleasant. He turned to motion for a refill and accidentally bumped the arm of the man standing next to him.

"Sorry," he said.

"You son of a bitch, you made me spill my whiskey," the man growled.

"I said I'm sorry, mister. I'll buy you another drink."

"I ought to pound the shit outa you," the man snarled.

Longarm took a closer look at him. The fellow was big. He stood a good three inches taller than Longarm and probably weighed in at two hundred fifty, not a bit of it fat.

"Look, I'm not going to say it again," Longarm told him. "Now let me buy you that drink an' forget about it."

Longarm looked down the bar to the gent in the apron. He raised two fingers and motioned toward his empty glass. The barman nodded and picked up a bottle and a pair of glasses.

The next thing Longarm knew, he was lying in the sawdust on the saloon floor, his head aching and his jaw feeling like it was broken.

"Wha—what the f-fuck?"

The bartender was kneeling at his side. "Are you all right, mister? Do you want me to call a doctor or somebody?"

"No, I . . . I think I'm all right," Longarm said. It was a struggle to sit up, but on the third try he managed. With the help of the bartender tugging on his arm.

"I was worried for a bit there, Marshal. You been out for a while."

"Really? Damn!"

"Stay there. I'll get you a beer or something."

"I think . . . can you help me up?"

"Yeah, sure. You aren't going to pass out or anything, are you?"

"No, I'll be all right. Just help me up. I'll be fine."

Longarm did not feel fine, but he wanted to stand on his own hind legs. Being on the floor was not his idea of a pleasant evening.

The bartender and another customer took Longarm's arms and helped him upright. He leaned against the bar and looked around. The big man who had sucker punched him was nowhere to be seen.

"Are you looking for Lennox?" the bartender asked from back on his own side of the bar. He set a whiskey glass and a beer in front of Longarm.

"He's the guy that punched me?" Longarm asked.

"Yes. His name is Lennox but I understand his friends call him Ox."

"The son of a bitch has friends?"

"At least one. That one told him who you are, and the both of them hustled out of here quick as rabbits. I guess they thought you might arrest Ox for assaulting a peace officer or something."

"I ought to," Longarm said, not meaning it. He kept personal grudges separate from the line of duty. "Bastard." He picked up the beer and took a deep swallow. The crisp lager tasted good. The whiskey he chased it with tasted even better. He cleared his throat and spat and finished the whiskey.

"Another?" the bartender asked.

Longarm shook his head. "No, I'd best quit now. My head feels bad enough without asking for a hangover on top of it. But I thank you for your kindness."

"My pleasure," the bartender said.

"How much do I owe you?" Longarm asked.

"Nothing. Those two are on the house."

"Thank you again." Longarm extended his hand. "For more than the drinks."

"Any time. Well, not for . . . uh . . ."

Longarm laughed. "No, not for that again." He found his Stetson. Someone had laid it on the bar. He put it on and touched the brim in silent salute, then headed for his room. He definitely wanted a bath after lying amid all that sawdust, and a solid night of sleep might help to quell the pounding in his head.

Chapter 12

Longarm awoke well before dawn. He felt considerably refreshed although his jaw ached like he had been kicked by a mule. And perhaps he had, at that.

He washed and dressed quickly and went downstairs and out into the chill of the predawn. The air felt good. The warmth in his belly from a hearty breakfast at the café felt even better.

Longarm presented himself at the Carver Express Company office in time to help Will put the four cobs into harness.

"Thanks, but you didn't have to do that," Charlise told him.

"Have to, no. Want to, yes," he said with a smile. "An' if you don't mind, I'll ride along on the run today. If nothin' else, it will give me an idea of what your route is like."

"Of course. Even if I didn't want you to ride, you have the right. That is specified in the mail contract. Federal officers have that right," the lady said. She turned and called out, "Will, Mr. Long will be your passenger today." Turning back to Longarm she asked, "Do you want to ride up top like a shotgun guard or inside the coach?"

"Up top, I think," he said. "I want t' be able to see as much as possible an' pester Will with questions when I think of 'em."

"Fine. Would you like a shotgun? I'm not expecting trouble, but the sight of you might keep any highwaymen away."

"Thanks, but no shotgun. If there's robbers laying in wait, I wouldn't want to keep the sons o' bitches away. I'd rather they come in where I can get to 'em and put a stop to this nonsense."

"All right then. We do have two passengers who are ticketed to Lake George. One of them is pretty," she said with a smile.

"But I bet she's not as pretty as you," Longarm told the lady.

Charlie began to blush. She turned away quickly and retreated into the safety of the office, Longarm grinning behind her.

Chapter 13

"Hyup, boys. Hyup!" Will snapped the popper on his whip above the ears of his near-side leader and the team stepped out, the coach swaying and lurching behind them.

Longarm grabbed hold of the rail beside the driver's perch. He had forgotten what it felt like to ride on top of a coach. The outfits were tall and ungainly and very badly sprung on leather slings. To the uninitiated, they felt like they might tip over sideways at any moment.

Will Carver chuckled at his side, evidently having seen Longarm's unintended grasp at safety. "You get used to it," he said with a smile.

"Either that or die of a heart attack," Longarm told him, only half joking. From up so high above the road, the side-to-side movement was exaggerated and felt dangerously uncontrolled.

"This morning," Will said, "we'll go down to Bailey first, then swing back through Lake George and Guffey before we come back north to Hartsel and Fairplay. Tomorrow we reverse that and go the other way around.

"There really isn't much point in going down through

Guffey. We almost never have any passengers going there or boarding down there, but the grade to make it up the bluff from the floor of South Park to the plateau where Lake George is, is just too much for the horses to manage. Too steep, that is. So we take the longer but easier route through Guffey."

Longarm nodded. He was still clinging to the iron railing as if his life depended on it. And Will was still laughing at him.

By the time they left the open ground around Fairplay and entered the pine forests above Bailey, Longarm was more comfortable on the driving seat. A little.

They pulled to a halt in front of a log building set amid a dozen others just like it, all of them shaded by the surrounding pines.

"This is the general store and post office," Will explained as a bearded man in bib overalls walked out the front door and nodded to the young man. His beard was so long it almost completely covered the blue denim bib. His dark hair was tousled and he was barefoot.

"This is Tom Rickets. He's the postmaster here." Will grinned. "Among other things. About the only thing Tom doesn't sell is women. He says you have to go out and find those on your own."

To the two passengers in the coach below, Will called, "This would be Bailey. We won't be stopping but a minute, so if you want to ride on to Lake George you'd best not get out."

Will handed a thin packet of letters down to Rickets and received a handful in return. He took a moment to sort the letters into the appropriate mail pouches then touched the brim of his hat and nodded to the Bailey postmaster.

Will picked up the driving lines of his team, but Rickets said, "Wait a minute, Will. You have a passenger going to Fairplay."

Rickets returned to his shack and led a young woman

out. It was obvious what the lady—girl, really—did for a living. She was all feathers and ruffles and gaudy face paint, and Longarm could smell her perfume from on top of the coach.

She carried a small valise. Rickets did not help her with it, and she was having trouble lifting it to the roof of the tall coach, so Longarm jumped down and took it from her.

"Thank you, sir." Her voice was barely a whisper, and when she climbed into the coach, she shied away from the other passengers as far as she could get and still be in the same cabin with them.

Longarm climbed back onto the driving box with Will and again took hold of the guardrail. But not with such a death grip this time. He was almost getting used to the swaying and bumping by now.

"This stretch from Bailey down to Lake George is where the highwaymen have been lying in wait," Will cautioned. "You might want to keep your eyes open now."

"Actually I've been keeping them closed," Longarm said, deadpan. "Out of stark terror caused by your driving."

"In that case I'm doing something right today," Will said, once again snapping his whip over the ears of his leader.

Chapter 14

They broke out of the pines on a long flat above a rickety cabin. Will removed his hat and ran a hand over his forehead. "Thank God," he said. "No highwaymen this time."

"I got t' admit," Longarm told him. "I'm disappointed."

Will gave him a look of shocked disbelief. "You *wanted* to be robbed?"

"Damn right," Longarm said, nodding. "I want t' see those jaspers in front o' my pistol. Put the bastards in cuffs and be done with this shit. I want t' put an end to these robbers, Will." He smiled. "Which is not to say I want you or your mom to be troubled. But I really was hoping they'd show themselves today."

"Well, if you put it that way, I have to agree," the young jehu said.

"When do we get to Lake George?" Longarm asked as the road curved toward the lonely shack.

Will laughed. "We're here."

"This?"

"Yep. This is it. There isn't really a town, just this general store. We have a corral out back where we keep the change

of horses. And over there is a sort of barracks. In wintertime
there are work crews up here cutting ice for the market down
on the flatlands. Manitou and Colorado Springs and places
like that. It's a wonder there is a lake up here considering
how much of it they haul away in the form of ice each year.
You'd think they would haul it all away one of these days. In
the meantime, you have Lake George. And Beaver."

"There's beaver in the lake?" Longarm asked, in-
credulous.

"No, of course not. The Beaver I'm talking about is Beaver
Jones. God knows what his real name is, or was. Everybody
knows him as just Beaver. He has the store up here. Maybe
someday Lake George will become a city but not yet."

Will drove the coach around to the back of the shack and
stopped beside a sturdy corral where four heavy-bodied cobs
stood swishing their tails.

He leaned out to the side and called down to the passengers, "All out for Lake George. And ma'am, you might want
to get out and stretch your, uh, limbs while I change horses.
It will be a half hour or so before we pull out for Fairplay."
He sat upright and turned to Longarm. "The folks going on
down to the flatlands wait here for the through coach. It comes
up Trout Creek Pass and Hartsel. I don't know what will happen when the railroad makes it on down the pass. There sure
won't be any reason to keep that coach running."

"Your route intersects with that one," Longarm said.

Will nodded. "Twice. Once here and once at Hartsel."

"That's what I thought. But why . . ."

"They run a six-horse hitch so they can make it up that
grade at the edge of the plateau. Even so if the coach is heavy
loaded, the passengers sometimes have to get out and walk
up. We only use four horses so it's much easier for us to go
down through Guffey and around that way."

"That makes sense," Longarm said.

Will climbed down to the ground and began unclipping the horses from his hitch. Longarm got down and helped him exchange that team for the horses waiting inside the corral.

"We have to fill the hay bunk, too," Will said, "and fill the water trough as well. Beaver doesn't do any of that, but he does allow us to use the corral."

"Where do you get your hay?" Longarm asked.

"There's a fellow, lives below Florissant. We contract with him to keep us supplied. Back home, of course, there's no problem finding hay. There are a number of outfits who cut hay on the flats around Fairplay and Hartsel. Grain, that's another story. It's no problem now that the railroad is running. We have it shipped up by rail nowadays." Will led one of the big horses out of the corral and began inspecting its hooves prior to putting the harness onto the animal.

Chapter 15

Charlie was standing outside the tiny express company head-
quarters when Will and Longarm pulled in that evening.

"So how was your trip, Marshal?" she asked, half teas-
ing and half serious about the inquiry.

"I enjoyed it just fine," Longarm said, climbing down
from the driving box. He looked up at Will and said, "I'll
be along in a minute. I want t' help you with the feeding and
cleaning up."

Will drove the coach around to the back of the office.
Longarm brushed himself off and turned to Charlie. "That's
a good boy you have there."

"Don't I know it," she said. "I wouldn't be able to make
it without him. He is a true blessing."

Longarm reached into his pocket for a cheroot, bit off
the twist, and lit his smoke. He eyed Charlie critically.

"Is there something wrong, Marshal?"

He smiled. "I'd kinda forgot what a fine-looking woman
you are, that's all."

"You also forgot that I can't abide smoke," she said,
ignoring the compliment.

"Oops. Sorry." Instead of putting the little cigar out, though, he stepped around to the other side of her so the breeze would carry his smoke away from the lady.

Charlie went inside the office—perhaps to get away from him and his smoke, although she did not say anything more to him about it—and he took a moment to admire the swish of the befeathered whore who had been their passenger since Bailey. That one looked like she would be a wild ride, the sort that made a man want to strap his spurs on extra tight before he mounted her. Not that he was interested in buying any female company at the moment.

Longarm finished his cheroot then walked around back, where he helped Will with currying the four horses and checking their feet, then feeding and watering all four of those plus the four others that would be used for the reverse route come morning.

And when all that was done, there was still harness to inspect, clean, and oil and the coach itself that had to be checked and the axles greased. Will even crawled beneath the big coach and looked at the thorough braces before he was satisfied that all was well.

"You treat those horses like they're your children," Longarm told him. "Hell, you treat them better than a good many men treat their human children."

"I just want to make sure things are as good as I can make them. I don't know if Mama told you, but we don't have so much of a margin that we can afford for anything to go wrong around here," Will said.

"She told me," Longarm said. "There isn't anything I can do to help you out with the company, but I sure as hell hope I can do something about these robberies."

"Join me for a drink?" Will said.

Longarm nodded. "With pleasure."

Chapter 16

Longarm spent the next several days riding on top of the stagecoach with Will Carver, but there was no sign of the highwaymen. He did, however, come to know and like the young driver. And he met the men Will dealt with along the Carver Express Company route.

On Sunday the coach remained parked behind the company office, while the horses stood quietly in their stalls.

Longarm slept late, past six o'clock, then rose and shaved. He bundled up his dirty clothes and carried them down to the Chinese laundry on his way to a café for breakfast.

He dawdled over a platter of beefsteak and fried potatoes then walked over to the sheriff's office to see if Bud Jahn had returned yet. He had not.

"I don't know when the sheriff will be back," Deputy Tommy Bitterman told him. "But, say, could you hold down this desk for a few minutes while I go take a leak? Please?"

"Sure, I can do that," Longarm said.

Bitterman disappeared almost before Longarm got the words out of his mouth. Longarm smiled. He had been in such a situation before and remembered well the discomfort.

He also knew better than to expect the deputy back in "a few minutes." Bitterman would take advantage of this respite for every bit as long as he thought he could get away with.

It was all fair game when a man was trapped on boring duty on a Sunday morning, Longarm knew, so he leaned back, crossed his legs, and lit a cheroot.

Two minutes later all hell broke loose.

Chapter 17

A young man came larruping into the sheriff's office, hat-less and breathless and wild-eyed.

"Where . . . where's Tommy?"

"I'm settin' in for him," Longarm said. "What's the matter?"

"A deputy. We're needing a deputy. There's . . . a fight. Somebody's gonna get killed, sure as shootin'."

Longarm came around in front of the desk. He was not sure what Sheriff Bud Jahn's rules were about leaving the place empty—there were prisoners in the jail back there, after all—but apparently this was an emergency. And any-way, Bud's rules were not Longarm's rules and his best judg-ment would just have to do.

"Show me," he barked, and the fellow turned and started back down the stairs at a good clip.

The fellow led the way to a saloon four blocks distant. Even before they arrived, Longarm could hear the commo-tion that was going on inside.

There must have been a dozen men or more involved in a wild melee. Fists were flying. Anyone on the floor was apt to get his head kicked in. Empty bottles, glass mugs, chairs, anything and everything constituted a weapon.

A man who Longarm assumed had to be the bartender— he was wearing a stained apron anyway—was down on the floor, bleeding heavily from a split in his scalp. It was obvious there was no one else interested in keeping order.

Longarm flipped his wallet open and hung it in the breast pocket of his coat with the badge showing bright and prominent. Then he waded into the fight, grabbing people by the scruff of the neck and hauling them upright, growling instruction for them to shut the fuck up and move aside, moving on to the next man.

He whittled the size of the fight down one by one until he came to the last man swinging. That one was the size of a small mountain. Or maybe not so small.

The fellow was huge. He was wearing shirtsleeves with only the sleeve garters holding them up because what remained of his shirt was hanging down around his waist. He was gleaming with sweat. And somehow he retained his hat, which was a soiled and much battered derby.

Tall as Longarm was, he had to look up when he confronted this one.

"Screw you, pipsqueak," the mountain roared as he lunged for Longarm's throat.

Longarm grabbed for his .45, reversed it so the flat of its butt was a club, and whacked the big man on the temple. The blow rattled him. Longarm could see that. But it did not put him down.

Longarm ducked under a wild sweep of the big fellow's right fist and whacked him again with the butt of the heavy revolver. This time his eyes crossed, but he still did not go down. Instead he swung at Longarm again.

This time Longarm did not quite get out of the way. The

fellow's fist landed like the kick of a mule. A rather large and angry mule.

Longarm felt things go fuzzy for a moment there. It was obvious he was not going to stand toe to toe with the big fellow, so he stepped in close and whacked him yet again. As hard and as solidly as he could manage.

The derby must have cushioned the blow to some extent, but Longarm gave it everything he had. And this time the fellow went down. It was like seeing a tree fall. His eyes rolled up in his head so there was nothing but white showing, and he toppled face forward, out before he ever hit the floor.

Longarm walked over to the bartender, who was sitting up with his back against the front of the bar—the wrong side for a bartender to be on, which he would undoubtedly agree with.

"Are you all right?"

The bartender looked up at him. It seemed to take the man a few moments for the fact of Longarm's presence to register and for him to see the badge that hung on the front of Longarm's coat. He shook his head and blinked. "I will be," he said.

"Want a hand up?"

"I . . . give me a minute."

"Sure," Longarm said, turning away to look over the room.

Two men in rough clothing were behind the bar drinking free whiskey as fast as they could gulp it down.

Longarm motioned them aside. They took a look at the badge and set the whiskey bottles down then scurried out from behind the bar.

Half a dozen other men were picking up chairs and slumping into them. A fair amount of blood was flowing. It probably was a good idea that the sawdust on the floor was thick and could absorb it all. Men were doing what they could to stanch the bleeding, but it was obvious that the local doctors would have some stitching to do.

The big fellow sat up, shaking his head. He looked up at Longarm. "Did you do this?"

"Uh-huh," Longarm told him. "D'you want to let be? Or would you like t' cool off in the jail instead?"

"You ain't taking me to jail now?"

"Not unless you need it," Longarm said.

The big man grinned. "Shee-it, mister, but you got a punch." Apparently he did not remember or had not seen that it was the butt of a clubbed revolver and not a fist that put him on the floor.

"I'm really not going to jail?"

"No, you're really not."

"Thanks, mister. I owe you one."

Longarm was not entirely sure how he meant that. Owed Longarm exactly what? Regardless, the fight had gone out of him now and he seemed willing to let it go, at least for the moment.

The bartender had climbed groggily to his feet and was back on the correct side of the bar for him. He sighed heavily and began assessing the damage.

Longarm waited around long enough to be reasonably sure that the party was over then hurried back to the sheriff's office, where he was supposed to be.

Chapter 18

True to Longarm's expectations—if not to his stated intention—Tommy Bitterman took his sweet time about returning to duty. It was the middle of the afternoon before the deputy returned and relieved Longarm from desk duty.

"Anything happen while I was away?" Bitterman asked.

Longarm snorted. "You know damn good and well there was a dust-up over at some slop joint. I don't even know the name of it. Anyway, I'm sure you know all about that an' did before you asked. Fairplay ain't so big a town that you won't have heard."

Bitterman's answer was a grin but not a single spoken word. Yes, he knew.

Longarm rose and reached for his hat.

"Did you make out a report about that fight over at Sanchez's place?" Bitterman asked.

"I don't do paperwork," Longarm said on his way out the door.

"Hey!" Bitterman barked. When Longarm was halfway

down the first flight of stairs, he heard the young deputy belatedly call, "Thanks." Longarm ignored him.

Longarm had a light lunch, then spent the afternoon idling at the bar in one saloon or another, not really drinking but keeping his ears open for any mention of the stagecoach robberies. The miners, enjoying a day off from their underground labors, were much more interested in the prizefight that was scheduled for that evening. There was considerable talk about that.

He had supper at a café on the east side of town, close to the railroad depot. When he walked out of the café, the sun was disappearing behind the peaks to the west. Darkness was gathering and there was a chill in the high mountain air.

He noticed a circle of torches and oil lamps with flaming wicks and bright reflectors on the far side of the railroad tracks. Crowds of men were gathering there, and a series of posts, connected with rope, had been set within the lighted circle.

That, he realized, was where the fight would be held.

What were the terms? He remembered hearing something about it when he first got to town. Five dollars to step into the ring, if he remembered correctly, and a hundred if you could last—five minutes, was that it?—if you could last five minutes without leaving your feet.

The promoter must be pretty confident of his boy if he was willing to lay a hundred on the line because surely there wouldn't be more than a handful of men who would want to climb into that ring. Five or six maybe, which meant the promoter and the fighter stood to earn only twenty or thirty dollars.

Of course, that was in entry fees. Side bets would be something else entirely. Longarm supposed that was where the promoter expected to make his money.

Regardless of all that, it should be a good show, especially for a town full of well-paid men who had little to do with their leisure hours except drink and go with the whores.

Longarm lit a cheroot and sauntered along with the growing crowd that was headed toward the lit-up ring.

Chapter 19

"Well, I'll be a son of a bitch," Longarm muttered under his breath.

The fighter was sitting on a three-legged stool in one corner of the ring. And why did they call it a ring anyway when it was always built in a square?

The man was stripped to the waist, already covered with a sheen of sweat that gleamed in the lamplight. Sweat? Or oil intended to cause the other man's leather gloves to slip aside?

Just that edge, tiny though it was, might sometimes be enough to make the difference, Longarm knew.

That sort of thing was common enough and, in fighting, was fair enough. But the thing that made Longarm's hackles rise was that this fighter in the ring was the same big son of a bitch who had sucker punched him in the saloon some days ago. Sucker punched him and knocked him out cold. His jaw still was sore when he chewed on the left side of his mouth.

And wasn't that almighty interesting.

Longarm felt a tightness across the width of his shoulders, and his breath came shallow and quick.

Almost involuntarily he flexed his hands, forming them into fists and then relaxing them again.

Five dollars, the entry fee was?

He had that much in his pocket.

Chapter 20

Longarm pushed his way through the gathering crowd until he found a place directly opposite Ox Lennox's corner. Then he stood, arms folded, and stared at the big son of a bitch who had knocked him cold with a sucker punch.

He wanted Lennox to see him, and inevitably Longarm's glare drew Ox's eyes to lock on with his.

It seemed odd, but if you stared at something, more often than not, that would draw the other's eyes to you. Hunters had long known this and avoided eye contact with their quarry. This time Longarm deliberately sent his anger across the twenty feet or so that separated him from Lennox. The bastard had knocked him cold when he was not expecting it and had in fact been trying to buy the man a drink to make up for the one he'd spilled.

Hunters had long known to avoid eye contact with their prey. Well, this time Lennox indeed was Custis Long's quarry.

Longarm just stood. And stared.

The crowd grew until it numbered several hundred men or thereabouts. Boys filtered through the noisy, boisterous crowd selling beer and peanuts. Men passed among the people taking bets. Whores flitted around the edges selling their own particular wares.

Eventually a small man in a tweed suit and yellow spats stepped into the ring and held up his hands for silence. Slowly the noise level abated as people became aware that things were about to commence.

"All right, everyone. My man here, Dexter Ox Lennox, will take on all comers. Five dollars to enter. If you can stay on your feet for five minutes, I will pay you a stack of lovely double eagles. Five of them. One hundred dollars, cash on the line. If you should happen to knock my man out cold, I will double that and pay two hundred. But I warn you. No one has ever managed to do that, and I don't expect to see it happen here tonight. Now tell me." The little man raised his voice to a shout. "Are you having fun?"

The answer was a roar of approval. "Let's go," someone shouted. "Get it going," another voice injected.

"And so we shall," the dapper little promoter said. "Now who will be the first to face Dexter?"

A burly fellow with bulging upper arms and practically no neck at all was the first to climb into the ring. He handed the announcer a coin and stripped off his coat and shirt. Likely he was an underground miner who swung a pick all day and could drive fence posts with his bare fists. At least he looked like that would be an ordinary feat for him.

"I'll go," he roared and motioned Lennox forward.

Lennox yawned—Longarm guessed he was faking it but wanted to give that impression—and took his time about leaving his stool, flexing his muscles, and marching into the center of the ring.

The fight, if it could be called that, was over before most of the crowd realized it had started.

The miner put his fists up.

Lennox pummeled the man's gut.

The miner doubled over.

Lennox delivered an uppercut that looked powerful enough to separate the fellow's head from his shoulders.

And that was the end of it, the miner flat on his back and Lennox, fists waving, taking a victory lap around the ring.

Longarm watched two more so-called matches. None of them lasted more than a minute. Every one of Lennox's opponents ended up sprawled in the dirt.

Finally Longarm stepped forward and crawled through the ropes, a five-dollar half eagle clutched in his hand.

Chapter 21

"I seen you before, little man," Lennox growled. "Where?"

"Hey, no jawing with the customers," his promoter put in, stepping between Longarm and Lennox with his palm up.

Longarm planted the five dollars into the man's hand and again glared at Lennox. But up close this time and with no doubt as to his feelings. "You cold-cocked me the other day. I want t' see how you handle it when a man is set an' ready."

"Oh, yeah. Now I remember," Lennox said.

"You'll remember even better after I whip your ass. I say you're yellow through an' through."

"Why, you—" Lennox did exactly as Longarm expected him to. He started a sentence but finished it with a wicked right hand.

Except Longarm was not standing there waiting to be punched. Seemingly effortlessly he swayed backward and Lennox's thundering right whiffed harmlessly past, only inches from Longarm's head.

The force of the blow pulled Lennox slightly off balance. Longarm stepped to the side and delivered a knuckles-forward punch to Lennox's right kidney.

If nothing else, Longarm thought, Dexter Lennox would be pissing blood for a few days.

Lennox's face turned red and he tried to drive an underhand blow to Longarm's gut. Again Longarm leaned back, pulling away just far enough to take the sting out of Lennox's punch.

"Hey!" Lennox bawled.

"Not used to having someone actually fight you?" Longarm taunted. He deliberately wanted to get under Ox's skin so the big man's anger would cloud his thinking.

Longarm reached out and with his thumb and forefinger took hold of Lennox's nose. He twisted the tip of the nose, and Ox howled with fury.

The big man lashed out with a flurry of lefts and rights, which Longarm dodged, swaying back and forth in time to the onslaught. Lennox's blows found thin air. Very thin air at this high mountain elevation. He was already beginning to gasp for breath.

"Hold still, you bastard," Lennox shrieked.

Longarm held still. Long enough to set his feet and deliver a right hand to the shelf of Lennox's jaw. The punch had his full weight behind it and should have been hard enough to drop an ox. This Ox indeed was jarred. Blood began to run from his mouth.

Longarm stepped in and gave the big man another shot with his right, this one on the point of Lennox's nose. Blood spurted into the air and began to drip onto Lennox's chest.

Lennox ripped a left hand low to Longarm's stomach and nearly doubled him over. Longarm, however, did not want to give Ox the satisfaction of knowing he had hurt him. Instead he stepped lightly to his right and threw a straight left into Lennox's breadbasket.

He heard the air whoosh out of Lennox's lungs. Moved right again and tattooed the other kidney.

Lennox straightened. He had gone pale and must have been in considerable pain. For a moment he seemed to forget where he was and what he was doing. He stood, back arched, jaw set.

It was a gift, and Longarm took it. He slid to the side a few inches to get the angle he wanted, braced his feet, and hit Dexter Lennox just as hard as Longarm had ever hit anything in his life.

Lennox's head snapped back and his eyes rolled up in his head until only the whites were showing.

The big man toppled face forward into the dirt, out before he ever hit the ground.

Longarm turned to the promoter and asked, "Do I have t' stand here long enough to finish out the five minutes, or will this be enough for the two o' you?"

It was only then that he became aware of the crowd noise. Men were screaming, cheering, some of them cussing.

Longarm grinned. It looked like somebody was going to be paying out big this evening—to him. He held his hand out to the promoter, palm upward. "Two hundred, I believe you said."

Chapter 22

Longarm turned to the crowd and shouted, "Drinks for everybody. Courtesy of Ox Lennox."

"Here, let me help you," a man standing next to him said.

"Thanks, but help me with what?"

"With that cut on your cheek," the fellow said, holding up a none too clean bandanna and wiping at Longarm's face. The cloth came away with blood on it.

"Shit," Longarm said, "I don't even remember being hit."

"He tagged you pretty good," the friendly fellow said, continuing to scrub at Longarm's cheek until he was satisfied that the blood had stopped seeping out.

That whole side of Longarm's face was numb and the side of his lips tingled as feeling returned.

Inside the ring Lennox was just beginning to come around. He looked confused. And thoroughly pissed off. The promoter helped him to his feet, where he remained upright but more than a little wobbly.

Lennox saw Longarm standing just outside the ring accepting congratulations from a good many of the crowd.

Congratulations and thanks for the round of free drinks that
the vendors were pouring as fast as they could.

The fighter made his way to that side of the ring and
leaned on the top rope to steady himself. "You bastard," he
complained. "We ain't gonna make a dime on this trip.
Might even go broke because o' you. Just don't turn your
back on me, that's all I got to say."

Longarm turned away from the well-wishers and told
Lennox, loudly enough for those nearby to hear, "I know
better'n to turn my back on you, mister, but if you come at
me, I'll either shoot you down or haul you off to jail for
assaulting an officer of the law. You got that?"

He did not have to say it twice. The promoter grabbed
Lennox by the arm and dragged him away before he could
get himself in any deeper.

Longarm returned to his conversations, making his way
slowly over to the drink vendors so he could use some of
his fight winnings to pay for all this pleasure.

And all the while he was keeping his ears open in the
hope of overhearing something—anything—that would
point to the identity of the mail thieves.

Chapter 23

Promptly at six the next morning Longarm was at the Carver Express corrals waiting for Will to join him and start the business of the day. There were already three passengers waiting out front for Will to hitch the team and get going.

The passengers were ticketed to Hartsel, where they would change to a coach heading down to Manitou and Colorado City. They could have made rail connections from Fairplay to Denver and then south to Colorado Springs, but it was actually quicker to go in a stagecoach down by the more direct route, quicker but in truth not as comfortable. The stagecoach connection was also much cheaper, and that might have been a consideration, too.

For whatever reason, they wanted to take the stagecoach route, and that would add a little income for Carver.

Longarm waited behind the express company office, laying out harness and in general starting the day's preparations, until he became concerned about Will. Finally, at six forty-five, he went inside. Charlise was there along with the few pieces of luggage going with the passengers and three packages consigned to Bailey.

"Any idea where Will is?" he asked the blond owner of the express company.

"No, I don't, and I'm starting to get worried about him," Charlie said.

"Doesn't he live with you?"

Charlie shook her head. "Will has his own place. He takes his meals with me, and he jokes about living with Mama but he's mostly on his own." She wrung her hands and walked over to peer out the front window. "This isn't like him, Marshal. I've never known him to be this late before. I haven't seen him since supper last night. He said he was going to the fight."

"I was at the fight but I didn't see Will. There was a big crowd, though. I could've missed him. If I knew where he lives—" Longarm began but was interrupted by the arrival of a scruffy little man in sleeve garters and an apron.

"Charlie!" the fellow said, out of breath and puffing from exertion. "Will insisted that I come tell you."

"Tell me what, Doc?" she asked.

"He's over at my clinic. He was hurt last night," the little man said.

"Hurt?"

"He doesn't want me to tell you, but . . . he was shot. Now don't get excited. He will be all right. But it will be a few days before he is up and around again."

Longarm stepped closer. "What happened?"

The doctor gave him a wary look. "It's all right, Doc," Charlie said. "He's a deputy United States marshal. You can tell him. And tell me, too."

"It was before the prizefight last evening," the doctor said. "Will was visiting, uh, he was visiting . . ."

"It's all right, Doc. I know all about Maybelle's and that Will likes to visit there sometimes."

"Yes, well, Will was at Maybelle's just like you guessed,

and he got into an argument. Not much of an argument the way I heard it. The other party pulled out a pistol and shot Will in the leg. He lost a lot of blood, but he will recover. It will be a few days before he can get out of bed, I think, and then he will be on crutches for a few weeks."

"Oh, Lord," Charlie said, turning pale. "Without Will . . ." She stood up straighter and braced herself. "I'll just have to do it all myself. But, oh, I don't know how to drive a team at all, much less a four-horse hitch."

"I know the route," Longarm said quickly. "I can drive until he gets upright again."

She gave him the sort of look he imagined a drowning man might give to his rescuer. "It would mean the difference between us staying in business or going under," she said.

"I want t' be on the coach anyway in order t' catch those mail robbers. After all, that's what I came up here for. This just puts me in a better position t' do my job. Now if you'll excuse me, I got to go make up that hitch an' bring the coach around to the front."

Chapter 24

It was a good thing Longarm had been paying attention when Will made up the team on those days the past week. Even so, it took him some time to sort out which horse should go where and how the various driving lines should be distributed. Finally he thought he had it right, hooked the traces, and climbed onto the top deck.

He took a deep breath and muttered a little prayer then took up contact with the horses' bits and shook the lines. "Hyup, boys. Hyup."

Damned if they didn't move out for him just like he knew what he was doing. Fortunately the team knew enough to make up for what Longarm lacked when it came to driving a four-up. But he knew good and well that if the team had been a six-horse hitch, he would have been worse than useless up there on the driving box.

He wheeled the coach around to the front of the Carver Express Company office and pulled to a halt there.

"Sorry for the delay, folks. We've had a little problem, but we're all right now. Let me help you with those bags, an' we'll get under way," he called down to the impatient and by now irate passengers.

He climbed down, loaded up the luggage and a package for the Bailey postmaster, helped the passengers into the coach, then made the climb up on top again.

Longarm tipped his hat to Charlise, who gave him a grateful look. Then he picked up the driving lines and, taking another deep breath, put the team in motion.

He was not sure about popping the whip to get them racing out of town. It would have ruined his day—and ruined the team for their future cooperation—if he accidentally nicked an ear with the popper, so he left the whip in its socket and drove with the lines alone.

It surprised him how much raw power was coming off those horses and being transmitted to his hands. Surprised him, too, how tiring the driving was, wearing on his shoulders and making his fingers ache.

Come nightfall, he was going to need a stiff drink and perhaps an application of liniment. Or two. Of each.

By the time they reached Guffey, he hoped the mail robbers would not show themselves during this trip because he was not at all certain he would be quick enough with his .45 to take them.

Come the next trip, he intended to bring a shotgun along, too. At least with a scattergun, you did not have to be as precise as with a revolver. There was room for error while still getting the job done. No wonder shotgun guards and stagecoach drivers carried the weapons they did, he thought.

And now he was a coach driver himself.

He safely delivered the passengers to Lake George and picked up two more there on their way over to Bailey, dropped them and the postmaster's package off there, and picked up two men and a matronly woman for the run back to Fairplay.

They pulled in at the Carver office in Fairplay well after dark.

But they, by damn, got the job done. Longarm felt good about that. And Charlie looked ecstatic.

"I was getting worried when it got dark and you still weren't here," she admitted while she helped Longarm break the hitch and tend to the horses for the night. "You must be hungry. Can I offer you supper as a way of saying thank you?" she suggested.

"I . . ." He was going to turn her down, then at the last moment changed his mind, and what came out of his mouth instead of a rejection was, "Yes. Thanks. That'd be nice o' you."

He set down the hoof he was working on and picked up another, certain that before this night was over, his back would break and he would be crippled for life.

Chapter 25

"That was wonderful, Charlie. Thank you," Longarm said, folding his napkin and laying it beside his now very empty plate. He smiled. "If you ever give up the stagecoach business, you could make it down in Denver as a high-class chef."

Her response was a loud, uninhibited guffaw.

"I have a question," she said.

"Shoot."

"Now I don't mean to give offense, but from the stiff way you are holding yourself, I'm going to guess that your back hurts. Am I right? Or am I right?" she said.

"You're right," he admitted. "Those boys pull hard, an' I'm not used to driving them. Haven't yet learned when to relax an' when to hold tight."

"Will's back gets like that sometimes, and he handles them every day. Would you like me to help you out with that?" she offered.

"If there's anything you know t' do short of shooting me to put me outa my misery, yeah, I'd appreciate it."

Longarm was thinking in terms of a few good shots of whiskey. Instead Charlise said, "Take your shirt off."

"What?"

"The shirt. Off."

"If you say so," he said and began fumbling at the buttons, his fingers still stiff from the day hanging on to those driving lines. He could scarcely imagine what it would have felt like had the Carver line run six-horse hitches.

Charlie helped him out of his vest and shirt, his coat already hanging by the door. She carefully folded both and laid them aside. "Now the gun belt if you don't mind."

Longarm complied, trying without success to hide a yawn.

"There is only one comfortable way to do this," she said. "I know from past experience with Will. You need to lie full length, facedown, and there is only one place in this little house where you can do that, so follow me, please."

He did, and Charlie led him past the kitchen to her bedroom. The bedclothes were surprisingly fluffy and girlish and the place smelled of powders and perfumes.

"There," she said. "On the bed, please."

Longarm did as she directed, stretching out facedown. Charlie perched on the side of the bed.

She picked up a small bottle and poured some of the contents into the palm of her hand.

"Don't worry," she said. "This is just a light oil. It isn't scented."

Longarm grunted his acceptance, and Charlie began smearing the oil onto his back. She oiled him with a liberal hand then began kneading his tight muscles with a relaxing, healing touch.

"Nice," he murmured at one point.

Then amazingly, he drifted off to sleep while Charlise Carver massaged him.

Chapter 26

When Longarm awoke, he was on his back and Charlie was tugging at his belt buckle. She already had his fly unbuttoned.

"You're awake," she said.

"Barely."

"There is something you should know. I am a widow. And a lusty woman. If that bothers you, now would be the time to get mad and storm out of here."

Longarm only smiled.

Charlie pulled his boots off and tugged his trousers down over his hips. When she saw the size of what he had to offer, she gasped. And smiled back.

She stood and quickly shed her dress and underclothes.

Charlise Carver was not a big woman, but she was nicely put together. She had full tits with protruding nipples and exceptionally large areolae. Her waist was small with a puffy vee of dark hair in her crotch. Her thighs were slender—he liked that—and failed to meet at the top.

He could see droplets of juice clinging to some of her pussy hair. The lady was more than ready.

She carefully folded each of her own garments and laid them aside then returned to again sit on the side of the bed, her hands falling quite naturally on his lower belly.

"It's beautiful," she said. He did not ask her what she meant by that. He was pretty sure he already knew.

Charlie's hand found his cock. Her fingers curled lightly around the shaft. She squeezed. Ran her hand up and down.

"If you don't stop that," he said, "you're gonna have a handful o' jism to clean up."

Charlie laughed. "There are worse things that could happen. Are you close to coming just from this little bit?"

"It's been a few days since I got laid," he admitted.

"Then let me take the pressure off. We can romp and play later, but for now . . ." She bent low and took him into the warmth of her mouth.

"D'you think . . . ah, that's nice . . . d'you think you can take it all? Just push on through int' your throat. Ah!" Longarm arched his back and cried out aloud as Charlise pressed down onto him, his cock filling her mouth and on into her throat.

He could feel the head pass through the ring of cartilage at the upper end of her throat. There was a slight resistance when it penetrated to that point, then it burst through.

Charlie gagged a little but she did not back off. She cupped his balls in her hand and, with one fingertip, lightly tickled his asshole.

Longarm was loving the feel of all this, but he could not hold back. Almost immediately he felt the gather of cum deep in his balls and then the quick, spurting release deep into her mouth.

Again he cried out aloud. Then collapsed onto Charlise Carver's feather bed.

There would be time enough for proper play—so to speak—later. But for now . . . it was good.

Chapter 27

Longarm lay still, enjoying the peaceful predawn. He had
gotten some sleep through the night. A little anyway. Now
Charlie lay on her back. Longarm was on his side, his legs
scissored in with hers, his dick filling her.

Charlie moved a little, then moaned. She proved to be
easily and deeply aroused, quick to reach her own climax
and quick to bring him to his.

Despite the full night of screwing, his dick was ramrod
stiff, with the kind of hard-on that made men claim a cat
couldn't scratch it. Longarm knew the expression but had
never actually attempted to see if it was true.

He moved his ass just enough to draw his cock to the
entrance of her pussy then rocked forward again, stroking
her a few inches at a time. Charlie's breath began to quicken
and her pussy lips fluttered and clenched as she reached
what must have been a powerful climax, at least judging
from the way she stiffened and gasped.

"Nice," he said.

"I agree," Charlie said, sitting up and swinging her legs off the side of the bed, "but it's coming on toward dawn. I need to open the office, and you need to make that hitch and bring the coach around front."

She stood and reached for her clothes. Longarm, too, left the bed. He helped himself to a splash of cleansing water from the pitcher and basin on a bedside stand, then he quickly got dressed, ready for the day. He needed to stop by the hotel and change to fresh clothing when he got time, he noted to himself, and he needed to pick up his clean clothes from the Chinese laundry.

Then he grinned silently to himself, thinking that neither of those routine chores was half as interesting as fucking Charlise Carver.

"We have time for breakfast," Charlie said. "I'll put some coffee on to boil if you run next door to the bakery for some crullers." She smiled. "Coffee and crullers. Always a perfect breakfast."

Longarm finished buckling his .45 in place and reached for his hat. "Back in five minutes," he said.

"Take your time. The coffee won't be ready quite that soon."

"In that case," he said, "I'll get the pastries an' then go around to start putting harness onto the boys. They don't know me yet, an' I sure don't know either them or the harness quite yet. You can tend to the coffee an' call me when you're ready to set down to eat."

Charlie nodded, rose onto her tiptoes to deliver a light kiss on the corner of his mouth, and went scurrying off to the stove to prepare their coffee.

Longarm stepped out back to the corrals and tried to remember which team of four he was supposed to drive this morning, reminding himself that today he ran the reverse route and started in Bailey then on around to the other way stations.

He genuinely hoped the Carvers would be able to make a go of the company. He liked both of them and wished them well.

Chapter 28

"You've been smoking again," Charlie said. "I can smell it on you."

"Yes, I have," Longarm agreed, "an' I intend to keep it up. Lady, I been smoking since I was knee-high to a grass-hopper. I ain't gonna change that now. Are these crullers all right? The fellow said they're fresh this morning."

"Hiram's baked goods are always fresh. Every evening he takes whatever is left over and gives them to the burros that work in the mines," Charlie said.

"Burros?"

"They work underground. They're of a good size to work in the tunnels, and their dispositions are better than bigger animals," she said.

"I had forgotten that," he admitted, reaching for a cruller.

"Wait. We need to pray first," she said, stopping his hand before it reached his mouth.

"Reckon I forgot that, too."

"Pray for an easy trip around and pray for Will to get back on his feet soon," Charlie said. "But I guess you aren't in the habit, so just do your praying silently and I'll do the same. It comes across either way, I've been told."

Longarm nodded and took Charlie's hand. He bowed his head and waited quietly until she gave his hand a squeeze to let him know she was done and they could begin eating.

After breakfast he went out back and finished building the hitch and pulled the coach around to the front of the Carver Express Company office.

Two passengers were waiting and another was making his way up the street.

It was time for the day to get started.

Chapter 29

"Well, now look what the cat dragged in," Longarm said with a smile as he pulled around to the corrals and found Will Carver waiting there to help with breaking the hitch and tending to the horses.

Not that Will was much real help. He was on crutches and could not do much. But he tried and he did what he could.

"Mom says you should come in to have supper with us when we're done here," Will said.

"Glad to. So how're you doing now?"

"Fair," Carver said. "Doc says I should be on crutches for a couple weeks, but it won't be that long. I figure I can take over driving again next week." He scuffed at the dirt with the toe of one boot, then looked up and reluctantly added, "But I have to admit that I'm hoping you will still be with us a little longer. Handling the horses on the ground and, well, and everything. It's a big help."

"I'll stay as long as I can, just so's you know that I have a job an' it comes first," Longarm said.

"Fair enough," Will told him. "And we do really appreciate all your help, both Mom and me."

"Good," Longarm said, hanging up the heavy harness that had come off the wheelers. "Then let's wash up before we go in to one o' your mom's fine meals."

Later, his belly full, Longarm gave Charlise a look and a nod to tell her he would be around after Will went back to his own place for the night. Then he turned to Will and said, "Let's go up front. Out there on the porch is the only place your mother lets me smoke. That woman is gonna drive me crazy with her evil ways." Past Will's shoulder he winked at Charlise.

Longarm led Will to a line of wicker bottom chairs beneath the front overhang, where in the mornings passengers could wait for the stagecoach to be brought around. The two of them settled into adjoining chairs, and Longarm reached for a cheroot. Will pulled out a plug of tobacco and bit off a chew.

When Longarm had his smoke lit, he leaned back and said, "Now you know not t' get into arguments with men who carry guns."

"An argument? Is that what you heard?" Will said. "It was no argument, Marshal. The truth is, I never saw who-ever it was that shot me."

"How'd that happen?" Longarm asked.

Will leaned forward and spat into the street, then said, "I was over at Maybelle's whorehouse. Two of the girls got into a fight." He laughed. "Oh, they were really going at it. Ripped each other's kimonos clean off so there they were, the both of them bare-assed, brawling like a couple kids in an after-school fight. Hissing and spitting and pulling hair. It was quite a show.

"Then I heard a pop, not half as loud as I might have expected, and my leg felt like somebody had whacked it with a maul. However it happened . . . maybe somebody's pistol went off by accident or something . . . but however it happened, my leg just buckled right out from under me, and I went down on my ass.

"I didn't even know that I'd been shot until my friend Anson saw that I was bleeding. I couldn't see the wound very well. It's up high on the back of my leg. Anson and some other fellows carried me over to Doc's place, and that damn doctor cut up my best pair of jeans to get to the wound. And now"—he indicated the crutches leaning on the chair beside his—"now I have this to deal with. I'll heal quick enough, but it's a nuisance for sure. My mom and me are grateful to you for your help, Marshal."

"Any idea how far away the gun was when you were shot?" Longarm asked.

Will shook his head. "No idea at all. Like I said, it must have been an accident. I mean, it wasn't like I was arguing with someone or that somebody might have a reason to shoot me. I was just standing there watching those girls fight. The next thing I knew, I was down on my back bleeding all over Maybelle's rug. Doc said I could have bled to death if Anson hadn't jumped in to help."

"Lucky," Longarm said.

"Very," Will fervently agreed.

Longarm took a long drag on his cheroot then closed his eyes and pondered the delightful things he intended to do with this young man's mother once Will went home for the night.

Chapter 30

Longarm went back to the Pickens House to sleep that night. Now that Will was up and around, it would not have been a good idea for him to sleep in Charlie's bed, pleasant though that was. He did dearly love waking up with a place to put his hard-on—and the place that Charlise Carver provided was very pleasant—but it simply was not possible any longer.

He did, however, make a two-hour visit to that bed after telling Will good night and seeing the young man off to his own digs.

Dawn found him with his belly warmed from the inside out by a heavy breakfast at the café, and he finally picked up his clean clothes from the Chinese laundry and stashed them in his room before going to the Carver office. He made up the hitch and drove the coach around to the front of the building to find Charlie waiting for him with coffee and four passengers, three going to Hartsel and one to Bailey.

Will was there, too. Longarm thought it a little odd that Will had not come around back to help with the horses. But then he was on crutches and might not find it so easy to get around. Besides, he needed all the sleep he could get. Longarm did not begrudge him a minute of it.

Will helped the passengers with their bags while Charlie chatted with them and Longarm drank her steaming hot black coffee.

When everything was in readiness, Longarm handed his almost empty cup back to Charlie and made the climb up to the driving box. He took up the lines and waited for Will to step aside, then cracked the whip—he had been practicing when he was alone out on the road—and put the team into their showy charge out of town and onto the road to Hartsel.

"You're getting better at handling the team," Charlie said that night as they lay in bed, both sweaty and spent from several hours of intense lovemaking.

She giggled and kissed his shoulder. "Keep it up and I might consider hiring you."

"As a driver?" he asked.

"No," she said playfully. "As a stud. Will can do the driving. You can stay in bed."

"Sounds like pleasant enough workin' conditions," he said. "What sort o' benefits d' you offer?"

"All the pussy you can eat," Charlie told him.

He laughed. "Now that's a job offer that tempts me."

Longarm sat up, stretched, and reached for the clothes he had discarded earlier in the evening.

His eye was drawn to a crack in the door. He was certain he had closed that door and set the latch before they came to bed.

Careful not to show his hand—though he was showing pretty much everything else from head to toe—he slipped out of the bed and casually lifted his .45 out of the holster he had hung on the bedpost.

Longarm reached the doorway in three strides. He brought the Colt up to the slight opening in one swift motion and yanked the door open.

Will Carver was standing there, red-faced with fury at the sight of the marshal in bed with his mother.

Longarm lowered the muzzle of his .45 and pulled the door the rest of the way open. "You might as well come in, kid, an' say what's on your mind."

Will broke into tears. He whirled around, clumsy on his crutches, and hobbled away as quickly as he could manage.

Chapter 31

They sat around the table in Charlie's tiny kitchen. Longarm was barefoot and shirtless. He had just thrown on some trousers before he ran and caught Will, forcibly bringing the young man back inside.

Charlise had a fluffy wrap but nothing beneath it. She was embarrassed but firm.

Will was visibly upset, his cheeks streaked where tears had flowed. He did not want to be there but acceded to his mother's insistence.

"You never loved Papa at all," he declared at one point. "If you did, you wouldn't be rutting like some common tramp with this . . . this man."

Longarm reached across the table and cuffed him. "Mind how you talk about your mama," he said.

Will gave him a sullen look but said nothing more.

Charlie tried to bring a measure of peace to the table. "We had some leftover coffee," she said. "It's heating. It will be ready in a few minutes."

"Listen to me, boy," Longarm said, peering directly into Will's face. "Your mama is a good woman. A nice person.

She's talked to me about your pap. She loved him very much. But he's gone now. Dead an' buried. And your mama is alive, with all the hopes an' dreams an' desires of anybody. Those desires include love, boy.

"I know you understand about sex. You go over to Maybelle's whorehouse from time to time. You romp with the ladies there an' think that makes you a man. Well, it don't. Being a man means letting other folks be who an' what they are.

"That, boy, would include your mama. She's a wonderful lady. An' I do mean lady. Don't you be bad-mouthing her or looking down on her for being a normal human person. It ain't your place to judge your mama. She gives you space to live pretty much the way you please, so give her the same courtesy."

Charlie left the table and returned with three heavy crockery mugs. She set them down and poured each full of coffee that was far from being hot. More like tepid.

Neither Longarm nor Will complained about the temperature. They drank the coffee more like it was medicine than for pleasure.

And perhaps it was Charlise's sort of medicine at that, Longarm thought. It gave them all pause to stop their condemnation and complaining long enough to let them calm down a little.

Charlie gave her son a cautionary look and said, "What were you doing peeping into my bedroom anyway?"

"I . . . I . . ." Will could not come up with any answer but silence.

"You were peeping at me. Your own mother. You are a peeper. If you weren't so big, I would take you over my knee and thrash you within an inch of your life."

Longarm looked away and tried to ignore the tirade that followed until finally a chastened Will left the table and skulked away.

"He'll be all right," Longarm said softly. "It ain't always easy for a boy t' come to grips with the notion that his parents are as randy as anyone else."

Charlie watched her son leave. Then she broke down in tears. Bad as this night had been for Will, it was just as unpleasant for his mother.

Longarm sat slowly sipping his now cold coffee, waiting for an opportunity to escape.

Chapter 32

The next morning, Sunday, he did not have to drive, so Longarm treated himself by staying in bed—alone—until past seven then got up and shaved, dressed, and went down the street to the café for breakfast.

Normally he would have wanted to spend time with the Carvers, but he suspected this would not be a good day for that. Mother and son needed time to work out their emotions and reach a measure of peace between them. It probably would be best for him to stay away, he thought, while they were doing that.

He could use a haircut, but the two barbers in Fairplay were closed for the day. Even the mines were shut down for the day of rest.

The churches were open, of course, but Longarm was not in the habit of attending services. That was not to say that he should not. He suspected that he probably should. But he did not.

The cafés and several fancy restaurants were open. But a man could only eat so much.

About the only other choice was a saloon.

So Longarm found himself helping to hold up the bar at
Ikey Tyler's Bearpaw Saloon—the full and correct name
for it according to the sign out front—along with a packed
house of customers enjoying their one day of rest for the
week.

"Say, you're that fellow that knocked out Lennox last
week, aren't you? Well, let me shake your hand, mister, and
buy you a drink."

It was a sentiment Longarm heard over and over during
the next several hours. By noon he was awash in cheap beer
and cheaper whiskey, to the point that he was feeling the
effects.

"Excuse me, gents. I have t' go out back an' make a con-
tribution," he said, disengaging from the boisterous crowd.

It was lunchtime but he was not at all hungry. Aside from
having the late breakfast, he had been munching on the free
lunch items available at Ikey Tyler's Bearpaw Saloon. Those
were even cheaper than the beer, but they filled a man's belly
and the heavy application of salt on everything contributed
to his thirst.

But then there was no such thing as a free lunch.

Longarm returned to the Pickens House and used the
outhouse behind the hotel then went inside.

"What can I do for you, Marshal?"

"I could use the tub an' some hot water to fill it," he said.

"Coming right up," Nathan told him. The desk clerk
turned his head and bellowed, "Johnny!"

Longarm hustled up to his room and stripped off his
clothing.

Chapter 33

Monday morning before dawn Longarm was back at the express company, busy building the hitch by the light of a lantern that was nearly out of oil so he had to work quickly before it sputtered out.

He looked up to see Will Carver working just as quickly on the other side of the rig. Will did not speak to him, very pointedly refraining from so much as acknowledging that Longarm existed. Longarm understood and took no offense. Will was still having trouble coming to grips with the fact that his mother was a sexual human being. And even more trouble accepting that Longarm was fucking her.

Between them they made short work of the routine tasks and had the day's team in place before the sun broached the horizon.

Longarm climbed up to the driving box and took the coach around to the front. Will grunted once but that was as close as he came to speech. He went inside when Longarm took the rig. He did not show himself to Longarm again that morning.

Charlise came out looking like she had not slept in two

days. And perhaps she had not. Her face was puffy from
crying, and her hair was unkept. Neither was at all like her.
Apparently, Longarm guessed, she and Will were still having their difficulties. Longarm did not envy either one of
them.

"I have some freight to go but no passengers this morning," she said.

At least Charlie was speaking to him, Longarm thought.
When he climbed down to load the packages consigned to
Bailey and one to Guffey as well, Charlie stepped close to
him and took him by the arm.

"Tonight," she said. "Come to supper, please."

"All right."

"You can stay the night if you like."

Longarm looked at her and raised an eyebrow.

"He doesn't like it, but I think he is beginning to understand," she said.

"Will he be at supper, too?"

"I don't know. I invited him. And I told him you would
be there."

"Did you say I'd be staying after?" Longarm asked.

Charlie nodded. "I did. He didn't like that, but I was telling him, not asking his permission. I think he understands
that much anyway."

"All right. I'll be there. I hope Will joins us."

"It's his choice."

Longarm gave Charlie a kiss then set in to loading the
packages.

Chapter 34

He made the deliveries, changed horses at Lake George, picked up five passengers in Hartsel, and arrived back in Fairplay well before dark.

Will Carver was there waiting to help break the hitch and tend to the horses. He again worked without speaking to Longarm.

When they were done, Longarm went back to the Pickens House to wash and change out of the dusty clothes he had worn on the road. He paused long enough to have a smoke before joining Charlie and her aversion to smoking then returned to the Carver office and Charlie's living quarters in the back.

Charlie greeted him with a kiss and a glass of whiskey.

"My two favorite things," he told her in response. Looking over Charlie's shoulder, he asked, "Is he here?"

Charlie shook her head. "No, but he promised me that he will be. If you don't mind, we should wait dinner for him. I have the table set for three and, well, I would just like to wait a little while. I know he will come."

"Of course we can wait," Longarm said. "But I tell you

what. I'd like t' have another o' those kisses and maybe another whiskey, too. Can you manage that?"

Charlie smiled and pressed herself against him, delivering a kiss that nearly sucked his tongue out of his mouth. And did get a good bit of it into her mouth.

"After dinner," she promised, her voice husky with desire.

Then she plucked his glass out of his hand and went to refill it.

Charlie stepped into her kitchen—or what passed for one in the living quarters—and began fussing with whatever was in the pot, so Longarm took his whiskey out to the front porch, where he could smoke without annoying the lady.

He was on his second cigar and his belly was rumbling with hunger when Charlie came outside. She sniffed the air and moved around to the upwind side of him.

"This isn't like Will," she said. "He promised, and Will always keeps his word. I don't know what could be keeping him. He is so late now that our dinner is ruined. It won't be fit to eat."

Longarm smiled and took her hand. "Darlin', you would be amazed at some of the stuff I've had to eat, like when I'm trailin' somebody and don't have no chance to buy proper grub. Proves I can eat 'most anything, so don't you be worrying about that. D'you have any idea what could've held him up this long?"

"No, I really don't. Custis, would you . . . I hate to ask you this, but could you stop at Maybelle's, um, house? He might be there."

"Why would you think that, if you don't mind me askin'?" Longarm said.

"He took some money from the box this morning, and I know that his rent is not due. That usually means he intends to visit the girls at Maybelle's," she said.

Longarm laughed. "You know the boy better'n he realizes, don't you?"

"I'm his mother, Custis. Of course I know him better than anyone." She smiled. "Including himself. Would you mind going over there?"

"Sure, no problem," he said, standing and stretching.

"One thing, though," Charlie said.

"Mmm?"

"Don't you *dare* get involved with those girls."

Longarm gave her a lingering kiss and said, "Not a chance. Not with what I got waitin' for me back here tonight." He gave her butt a quick squeeze and stepped down off the porch to head for Maybelle's house of ill repute.

Chapter 35

House of ill repute might be what a whorehouse was called in polite company, but that reputation did not curb their popularity. This one was certainly popular. When Longarm got there, Maybelle's was packed. Miners, businessmen, and cowhands crowded the place, everyone trying to talk at once, and the girls snatched up and sent back to their rooms—not alone—as soon as they set foot into the parlor.

"Marshal Long. How nice to see you in our happy home," a painted older woman, presumably Maybelle herself, said when Longarm walked in. He was not at all surprised that the woman knew who he was. A woman in this business would make it her business to know everything that went on around her.

"My pleasure," he said, tipping his hat and bowing slightly. "Though I have t' admit that I'm here on business, not pleasure."

She laughed. "I am very sorry to hear that, Marshal. I was going to recommend one of our nicest girls for you. If you change your mind, I can even get you in to see her ahead of the crowd."

"You're very kind. Perhaps another time, eh? In the meantime, have you seen young Will Carver this evening?"

"Will? No, he hasn't been in today."

"I know he planned to visit you," Longarm said. "Does he have a favorite girl? She might know something."

"No favorite. Will plays the field. He spreads himself around mostly. But two of his friends are here. Would you like for me to introduce them?"

"I'd like that very much," Longarm said.

"Would you like a drink while I go find them?" the old bawd offered.

"No, but thank you for the offer."

"Wait here. I won't be but a minute." She turned and disappeared into the mass of horny men in her parlor, leaving Longarm to wait in the foyer.

Good to her word, the woman returned in only a few minutes. She had a thin young man of about Will's age with her. He had pale hair, already receding despite his youth. He looked like a clerk of some sort but might have been anyone or anything for all Longarm knew.

"Marshal Long, this is Jesse Moore. Another of Will's friends, Jimmy Cranston, is here this evening but at the moment he is, um, occupied with my Abigail. Do you want me to bring him out anyway?"

Longarm shook his head. "I don't imagine that will be necessary, but thank you." He turned to the young man with Maybelle and said, "I'm looking for Will Carver. His mother is worried about him and so am I. Do you know where he is?"

Moore said, "No, sir. Will was supposed to meet us here this afternoon. He never showed up. We're both kinda worried about him, but we thought he went over to his mother's place early. He said something about having supper with her. He usually does that. So we just assumed he was over there when he didn't show here."

"No, I've been over there waiting for him with her. Any idea where he might be?" Longarm said.

"No, sir, I don't," Moore said.

"You know where he lives, don't you?"

"Yes, sir, of course."

"Would you show me, please?"

Moore glanced back toward the parlor. Then he sighed and said, "I was next in line to get me a girl."

Longarm motioned to Maybelle, who was hovering in the doorway to the parlor and pretending not to listen. Perhaps she really was ignoring the conversation.

"Excuse me, but Jesse here is next in line for a girl, an' I'm wanting him to help me with something. If I take him away for a few minutes, can you see that he gets some extra special service when he gets back, please."

"I can do that for you, Marshal." She looked at Jesse and smiled. "Help the marshal and I'll see that you get double time with Sandi, Jesse."

The boy's eyes nearly bugged out of their sockets, and Longarm guessed that Sandi was someone rare and special. Certainly Jesse seemed pleased by the prospect. The bulge at the front of his trousers attested to that.

"Let's go, Marshal," he said and headed for the door.

Chapter 36

Will Carver lived in a tiny shack on the north edge of Fair-play, set amid a half-dozen more just like it, all of them probably owned by the same man, or corporation, and almost certainly built at the same time to the same design.

From Maybelle's, it was only about a two-minute walk. Convenient, Longarm thought, much more so than the several other whorehouses that he knew about in or near the town.

"This one," Moore said, pointing.

Will's friend took the flagstone steps leading up to the door and reached for the doorknob. He barely touched the knob when he jerked back as if the metal were burning hot.

"What's the matter?" Longarm asked.

"I heard . . . I thought I heard something . . . something inside," Moore said.

"Move aside an' let me see," Longarm told the young man. He shouldered past Moore and took hold of the brass knob.

There was nothing wrong with the doorknob, but Long-arm, too, heard something inside. And unlike Jesse, Longarm knew what it was.

Someone in there was moaning in pain.

Longarm tried the door but it was locked. He studied the cheap lock for a moment, then took out his pocketknife and opened the sturdy main blade. He slipped that between the door and the frame and made contact with the lock bar.

Pressing forward to give the tip of the blade some purchase on the cheap steel of the lock, he prised the bar sideways until it cleared the mortise. The door swung open easily after that.

The room inside was dark but the moaning continued to come from it. Longarm reached into his vest pocket for a match and snapped it aflame with his thumbnail.

He strode forward, found a lamp in the middle of a small table, and lit it. Lamplight flooded the tiny room to disclose Will Carver, his face a pulped mass of blood, lying on the floor in front of the fireplace.

Jesse Moore rushed past Longarm and dropped to his knees beside his friend.

"Let's get him on the bed, Jesse. Help me," Longarm said. "An' be careful t' lift him easy. We don't know if there's any bones broke."

Between them, Jesse and Longarm were able to lift Will off the floor and deposit him onto his cot.

Someone, Longarm saw, had beaten the shit out of Will. Literally. It stank. But after a beating like Will had received, Longarm did not really blame him for that.

"Jesse, do me a favor. Go fetch Will's mother. She'll want t' be the one to tend him, I think."

"Yes, sir. Right away." Jesse raced off into the night, and Longarm bent close to Will in order to hear anything young Carver had to say.

Chapter 37

Charlise threw herself into action much as Longarm had expected she would. There was no better nurse than one's own mother, he thought as he watched Charlie soothe and clean and salve her son.

Longarm left the boy to his mother and buttonholed Jesse Moore before he could escape into the night. Jesse was obviously uncomfortable and itching to get away.

"Not so fast, son," Longarm said, his voice low and calm. "I got something t' ask you."

"Yes, sir?"

"D'you know two fellows named Ron and Craig? Who would they be?" Longarm asked.

"I know them. I don't much like them, but I know them. Ron is Ron Javit, or maybe it's Jabit. I'm not sure about that. Craig would be Craig Willborne. The two of them run together."

"Tell me about them," Longarm ordered, holding on to Jesse's upper arm to keep him from sidling away.

Jesse shrugged. "They're just . . . fellows. They live in town here. I see them a lot at Maybelle's. Ron is a carpenter.

Works on houses and shoring timbers in the mines, things like that. Craig works for Dayson's Feed and Seed. They, well, it's obvious what they sell. Like I said, the two of them run together. Are they the ones that beat Will?"

Longarm nodded. "They are. Will was able to tell me. Any idea why they'd go and do a thing like that?"

"I know there was some bad blood between them. Last payday there was a falling-out, I suppose you'd say. One of the whores at Maybelle's is a girl who calls herself Sweetie. She's sweet on Will. She went to him. Ron claimed he was next in line for her. He likes her a lot, you see. Him and Will got into a shouting match over her, and she refused to go with Ron. She insisted she was going with Will next or with nobody at all. And she did. She took Will upstairs and spent a lot of time with him there. Ron didn't like that at all but he didn't actually do anything about it. Not at Maybelle's. Anybody who causes trouble there, she'll post them, won't let them back in for a month. One man she actually banished permanent. Nobody wants to risk that, so things are generally pretty orderly at Maybelle's. That's all I know, Marshal. Can I go now. Please?"

Longarm nodded and let go of the young man. Jesse hurried away while he had the chance.

Charlie seemed to have things under control. She had washed the blood off Will, and he did not look as bad now as he had to begin with. Longarm did not think Will's injuries were the sort that would require the doctor.

"If you'll excuse me, there's something I got t' do," he said, not at all sure that Charlie heard. She was concentrating completely on her injured son. Longarm touched the brim of his Stetson to her regardless, then slipped out into the cool of the evening.

Chapter 38

"Nice to see you again, Marshal," Maybelle said. "What can I do for you?"

"I'm looking for a couple fellows, ma'am," Longarm said, touching the brim of his Stetson. "Fellows name of Ron Javit and Craig Willborne. Do they happen t' be here tonight?"

"That would be Ronny Jabit and Craig Willborne. I know them, of course, but they haven't been in this evening. I haven't seen them for several days," the old madam said.

"Any idea where I might find the two of 'em?" Longarm asked.

"Just a minute, Marshal." Maybelle turned and motioned to a young woman, who hurried to join them. The girl was thin and had acne marring a pouty face. At the moment she was wearing a professionally insincere smile.

"Yes'm." She fluttered her eyelashes at Longarm, obviously taking him for a customer.

"Find Pansy and tell her I want to see her," Maybelle said.

The smile disappeared the moment she knew the tall, handsome gentleman was not a customer who wanted her.

"Yes'm," she repeated, then turned and left but at a much slower pace than before.

The girl went into the crowded parlor. Shortly afterward a tall girl wearing a pink kimono came out. "You wanted to see me, ma'am?"

"Ronny Jabit and Craig Willborne. Have you seen them lately?"

"Last Saturday night, I think," the girl said.

"Do you know where they might be this evening?" Maybelle asked.

"I know they like to do their drinking in the loft over at Dayson's. Craig has a key to let them in. They like to buy a bottle and carry it up into the hay loft. It's private. I think . . ." She shot a look toward Longarm.

"It's all right," Maybelle said. "Say whatever you were thinking."

"Yes, ma'am. I think they might bugger each other up there when they can't afford to come here," Pansy said. "I don't know that, mind. But it's what I think."

"Thank you, dear. You can go now."

The girl turned and went back to the customers in the parlor. Maybelle waited until she was gone, then said to Longarm, "Is there anything else I can help you with, Marshal?"

"No. You've been a big help, an' I thank you." He smiled and added, "I guess there is one more thing after all. Where can I find Dayson's feed store?"

Chapter 39

Dayson's Feed and Seed was on the southeast side of town. Longarm found it with no problem. It appeared to be dark inside, but . . .

The front door was unlocked. Longarm let himself in.

The interior of the building had the sweetly musty scents of fresh hay and the mixed grains that were needed by the myriad draft stock used to carry ore, tools, foodstuffs, and anything in between.

A very faint light showed in the loft overhead. The idiots were up there drinking, lounging on the hay, and burning something, a candle or a small lamp. Either one was a danger to life and property.

He could hear a low buzz of conversation above.

Longarm felt his way to the ladder leading up to the thin, yellow smear of light coming from the trapdoor into the loft.

The dry wood of the ladder creaked under his weight, but the two loafing in the loft with their bottle apparently heard nothing. Certainly they were unaware of his presence when Longarm climbed up and joined them.

"Who the hell are you?" one of them demanded.

The other, the larger of the pair, said, "I know who he is, Ronny. Son of a bitch is that deputy marshal from down Denver way. Up here somethin' to do with the robberies."

"Well, fuck you, Marshal," Jabit said cheerfully. "Want a drink? Mind if I have one m'self?" He tipped the bottle up and drank from it. There was enough light to show that the two of them had already put a rather severe dent in the contents of their whiskey bottle.

"What d'you want up here, Marshal?" Willborne asked. He did not sound quite as drunk as his companion was.

Longarm was very pleased to see that, Pansy's suspicions notwithstanding, both Jabit and Willborne were fully dressed and their flies were buttoned. He did not know what-all they liked to do up here when they were alone, but at least he had not interrupted anything.

"Yeah," Jabit said. "What d'you want with us? We ain't done nothing."

"You bothered a friend of mine," Longarm said, his voice mild and almost pleasant.

"We did?"

"Uh-huh. You fucked with Will Carver. Ganged up on him an' beat him pretty bad," Longarm said, his voice becoming even more cheerful as he looked forward to the task he had come up here to perform. "You shouldn't ought to do something like that, boys. It pisses me off something awful. An' you shouldn't do that neither."

"Now wait," Willborne said, sitting upright and setting the whiskey bottle aside. "Wait just a minute there."

Smiling broadly, Longarm stepped toward the two.

Chapter 40

"How is he?"

"Oh. Hello, Custis. I didn't hear you come in."

"Is Will all right?" Longarm asked.

"He will be," Charlise said. "I cleaned him up as best I could and put some salve on the cuts. I hope that's all right. It's the salve I use for the horses."

"I'm sure it's just fine," Longarm said.

"Oh, look there. You've skinned your hands up something awful. What happened?"

Longarm shrugged. "Nothin' important."

"Well, let me see them." Charlie took his hands in hers and examined them closely. "Let me put some of that salve on them. You don't want them to get infected. Nor to stiffen up. Don't forget, you need to drive in the morning. And Will won't be in any condition to help you tomorrow. I can come out and help with the harnesses, but if there are any passengers, I'll have to collect their fares. Same thing if there is freight for you to carry. I'll have to check it in and collect the money for them. I'm afraid I won't be much of a help for you."

"That's all right," Longarm said. "Those horses an' me get along just fine. We've got used to each other."

"Mama. Mama?" Will's voice was thin.

Charlie did not bother excusing herself. She turned and hurried back inside, leaving Longarm standing in the chilly night air.

He smiled, not at all offended that she had forgotten her intention to put salve on his badly skinned-up hands. Will came first in his mother's concern, and that was as it should be.

Longarm turned and headed for the café close to the Pickens House so he could quell the rumbling in his empty stomach. Dinner was another thing that had slipped Charlie's mind this evening.

Chapter 41

Longarm borrowed a fingerful of grease—probably pork, but that was unimportant—from the café and took it back to his room. He spread the grease heavily over the cuts on his hands, wincing as the salt contained there reached the open flesh. It stung like a son of a bitch, and his first inclination was to wash it off. He did not, and after a minute or so the stinging lessened to a bearable level.

He unloaded his .45 and spent another few minutes drawing, cocking, and aiming it. But not pulling the trigger as dry-firing could damage a revolver.

When he felt that his hands were limber and quick enough, he reloaded the Colt and hung his holster on the bed post. Then, and only then, did he feel he was ready to go to bed.

He slept well and woke early, ate a heavy breakfast at the same café, stopped into a nearby outhouse for a satisfying morning shit, then headed for the Carver office.

He went around back to the corrals, pulled out the team for the day's run, and set about the work of harnessing and hitching them. He was perhaps halfway through the process when Charlise showed up and began to help.

She worked but did not speak, and when they were close to finishing, he asked, "Are you pissed off or somethin'? You've hardly spoke two words since you come out here this mornin'."

"No, Custis, I'm not angry. I'm worried."

"'Bout Will?" It was a silly question, he supposed, but he asked it anyway.

"Yes. And about the company. You can't help us out forever. You will find those robbers and go back to Denver, or else you will simply give up and go home. Either way, we won't be getting this free help very much longer. Now this mess with Will. What if he can't drive again? Or doesn't want to?"

Longarm hooked the team into the traces and leaned against the coach. He pulled out a cheroot—surely Charlie could not object to him smoking outdoors—and lit it.

"He wasn't hurt that bad," Longarm said.

"No, but last night he was talking about maybe we should just give up and close the line. Move down to Manitou or something. I think . . . there are practically no girls his own age up here. Not except for the girls at Maybelle's and places like that. He visits those, but they are not the same as having a proper girl, a decent girl," Charlie said.

Then she shook off her worries and in a crisp, no-nonsense voice said, "Three packages for Bailey today, two for Lake George, and three passengers, all going to Bailey."

Longarm took the hint and made the climb up to the driving box. He took up the lines and clucked the team into motion.

His day was under way.

Chapter 42

Longarm rolled back into Fairplay with a flourish, the big horses at a run, knowing they were on their way to rest and a good bait of grain.

His hands hurt pretty bad, but that was only to be expected. It occurred to him as he was dismounting from the tall coach that his forearms no longer ached from the strain of driving. He was becoming accustomed to it now.

There was one passenger aboard so Longarm stopped in front of the office to let the man off.

"Thanks for travelin' with us," he said as politely as he knew how—that was the way employees were supposed to act, wasn't it?—and touched the brim of his Stetson to the man. The passenger ignored Longarm, collected his bag from the trunk, and walked away.

Longarm had been prepared to help the surly son of a bitch with the bag, but if he wanted to act like that, the hell with him. Instead he sat on the seat—it badly needed a pillow or something to pad the pounding—and lit a cheroot, then drove around back and began breaking down the hitch.

"Will you come to supper?"

He looked up from the work. He had not noticed Charlise come out.

Longarm nodded. "Glad to. Mind if I stop by a store before supper, though? There's some things I need t' buy, cigars an' soap an' such, and the places might be shut by the time we get done."

"I should hope so," Charlie said with a smile. "I intend to work you hard tonight."

Longarm grinned. "Promise?"

"Promise."

"Now that's the best news I've had all day."

"Tough day?"

"Nothing in particular. How's Will?"

"Sore," she said.

"I'd be amazed if he wasn't."

"He will be taking supper with us."

Longarm nodded. "O' course he should. You're his mother an' he needs you."

"You don't mind?" she asked.

"Oh, hell, Charlie, I don't mind. I'm not the one got my nose outa joint, you know."

She brightened. "Good. Now go do your shopping." She wrinkled her nose. "And wash up. You smell like horses and road dust. I'll have supper on the table in an hour."

"Sounds fine." He walked around the coach, took the woman into his arms and kissed her, looked around to make sure no one was nearby, and groped the lady's ass. "Until later," he said.

Chapter 43

"Wonderful dinner," Longarm said, pushing back from the table.

"I agree, Mama. It was great," Will added. Then hesitantly, he said, "Can I ask you something, Marshal?"

"Of course," Longarm said. He was a little surprised, though. Throughout the meal Will had been mostly silent. Longarm assumed that was because of his injuries. But perhaps not. Will sounded now like he had something very serious on his mind.

"I want to ask you . . . that is to say . . . Mama told me about your hands being all banged up. I see now that they are. And, well, I was wondering . . . would you happen to know anything about how Ron and Craig got torn all to pieces the other night?"

"They did, dear? You never mentioned that," Charlie said.

Will looked at his mother. "Both of them. Ron has a broken jaw, maybe some other stuff, too. And Craig has his arms broken. Both of them. They're in splints." Will snickered and said, "With both arms in splints, he's gonna have to ask for help if he wants to wipe himself. I mean . . . I shouldn't say that in polite company, I guess. But it's true. Anyway, Marshal, what would you know about that?"

"Me? Whyever would you ask me a thing like that?" Longarm laughed. And reached for his coffee cup.

"Look, I know as good as you do what happened," Will said. "Well, sort of. I don't know the details, and I'll bet neither of them would admit to it. But I know what happened with them, and I want to thank you for standing up for me. Nobody but my mama has ever done that for me, not ever before, and I appreciate it."

Longarm acted like he had not heard. "This is fine coffee, Charlie. Thanks."

She looked from her son to Longarm then said, "If you want to light one of those stinking cigars of yours, I won't make you take it outside."

"I don't mind smoking out front," Longarm said, standing and picking up his coffee cup. "If you don't mind, I'll help myself to a refill and carry my cup out front before I light one of my, as you put it, stinking cigars."

He stepped around to the other side of the table, leaned down, and gave Charlise a long, deep kiss. Then he winked at her and headed out front.

Behind him he heard Will's chair slide back over the puncheon floor.

"I'll take mine out there, too, Mama."

Longarm smiled. Apparently all was right with the world.

Chapter 44

"Good night, sweetheart." Charlie gave Will a hug and a kiss.

"G'night, Will," Longarm said.

"Good night, sir. I'll see you in the morning. I can help with the horses, I think."

"You're still a little wobbly on your feet," Longarm said. "Let me take care of it for another day or two. Then we'll see. Tomorrow morning, you just sleep in. Enjoy it while you can."

Will gave Longarm a smile and his mother a kiss and another hug then set off for his own home.

Longarm turned to Charlise and said, "I could use some o' that hugging an' kissing if you got some t' spare."

She came into his arms. "I think I can manage that."

Charlie was naked by the time they reached the bedroom, and Longarm was not far off that mark.

He kissed her thoroughly then began licking her nipples and lightly sucking them. Charlie moaned and began to writhe, her hips gyrating, her hands running through Longarm's hair.

He moved lower, licking her belly, running his tongue
through the mat of hair at her crotch and finding the now
wet and slippery lips that guarded her tiny, engorged clit.

Charlie cried out aloud when he began to lick that. She
clenched and trembled as she came and pushed him away.
"Too powerful," she said. "Now let me, dear."

Longarm lay back on the bed and closed his eyes, concentrating on the feelings Charlie was giving him.

She began by running her tongue into his ear. Then down,
across his neck and upper chest, to lick his nipples, the sen-
sation running down into his belly like an electric shock.
She licked him thoroughly then ran her tongue down over
his belly.

Charlie carefully licked his cock, running her tongue up
and down, peeling his foreskin back and circling the head of
his prick with her tongue before taking his dick into her mouth.

She sucked him, then pushed deep into her mouth, deeper
into her throat.

Longarm arched his back, took hold of Charlie's ass, and
squeezed.

"If you don't . . . back off . . . I'll . . . come in your
mouth," he panted.

Charlie did not back off.

He felt the gather and rush of his cum. Felt the explosion
of sheer pleasure as his fluids built up deep in his balls and
shot out through the length of his dick to burst forth inside
Charlie's throat.

She cupped his balls and continued to suck and to swallow until she was satisfied that she had gotten it all. Then,
smiling, she sat up.

"That takes the edge off both of us," she said. Then,
laughing, she added, "Now we can get down to some serious fucking."

Chapter 45

Longarm woke up early. Charlie lay on her side, her butt pressed warm against his side. He rolled to face her and slid his erection between her legs from behind.

She woke up slowly and began to press herself against him while Longarm slowly, gently stroked in and out.

Charlie came first, then he spewed his seed into her body.

"Nice," she mumbled.

"Agreed," he said.

She picked up the washcloth she had placed on the bedside stand and wiped the spent jism from him then pressed the cloth between her legs to catch any cum that seeped out of her pussy.

"Take your time," she said, rising from the warmth of the bed. "I'll start breakfast."

Longarm got up, washed, and dressed. He could hear Charlie in the kitchen as she rekindled the fire in the stove and put coffee and a skillet on to heat.

By the time he went out back for a morning shit and

washed up again, she had bacon sizzling in the skillet and coffee perking in the pot.

"Nice," he said, kissing the back of her neck.

It occurred to him that this very pleasant, very domestic morning might lead Charlise Carver to think in terms of a permanent relationship. He hoped she did not. When this job was over, he would be heading back down to Denver and the United States Marshal's Office. He hoped she understood that.

It probably would be a good idea for him to return to the Pickens House to sleep from now on.

Will joined them for breakfast then went out back with Longarm to help put the cobs in harness for the day's work. He seemed cheerful and pleasant and no longer resentful of Longarm's relationship with his mother.

"Give me another couple days and I'll be able to drive again," he said, scratching the sensitive hollow beneath the near leader's jaw. It was obvious from the way he handled the horses—and from the way they responded to him— that Will was fond of each of the big boys that pulled his coach.

"Whenever you feel up to it," Longarm said. "No need for you t' be in a hurry, though. I don't mind the drivin', especially since I got t' be there anyway the next time those jaspers try an' take the mail."

Longarm drove around to the front of the building and loaded a number of small packages consigned to Bailey, one to Lake George, and one to Guffey as well. There were no passengers. He had to wait a few minutes, though, for Postmaster Jon Willoughby to show up with the day's mail.

When he did come around, there were pouches for Bailey and Lake George, nothing for Guffey or Hartsel.

"Is that it?" he asked Charlie.

She was standing on the porch. Will was with her.

"That's everything."

Longarm popped the whip over the ears of the off leader, and the team surged into motion.

Chapter 46

In Bailey he swapped their pouch for a slim packet of letters going down to Denver. Those he would carry back to Fairplay, where they would be put on a train. There was also one letter going to a Colorado Springs address. That one would be left at Lake George to be picked up there and carried down Ute Pass to the flatlands below.

"Thanks, Tom," Longarm told the Bailey postmaster.

"Mind if I ask a question?" Rickets said, standing at the side of the tall coach and looking up at Longarm.

"No, go ahead." The coach was on schedule and the horses could use the breather before they started the run through the forest to Lake George.

"Will you be driving permanent now? I don't mean to pry, but I'm seeing you kind of regular nowadays. It has me to wondering," Rickets said.

Longarm smiled and shook his head. "No, I won't. Young Will got hurt. I'm just filling in temporary until he's up to driving again. He should be back up here in another few days, I think."

"Thanks. I was just, you know, curious about that. Hope you don't mind the question."

"I don't mind at all, Tom. It's no secret," Longarm said.

"Something else then if you don't mind another question."

"Go ahead."

"The prizefight a little while back. Was it really you that whipped Ox Lennox?"

Longarm laughed. "Guilty," he said.

Rickets turned away, chuckling, and Longarm made contact with the bits of his team and popped the whip over his leaders' ears.

The coach took off with a lurch and set out along the now familiar road.

Chapter 47

"Dammit, Charlie. Just dammit t' hell anyhow." Longarm looked like he was close to breaking into tears of frustration. He took his hat off and slammed it down on the table. "Dammit," he howled.

"I was this close," he said. "Saw them plain as day. The two of them there was. Standing off to the two sides o' the road, one o' them on either side. Wearing dusters head to toe. And big hats that kept me from seein' anything of their faces. Bastards likely was wearing flour sacks or bandannas or the like. I couldn't tell what.

"But, oh, I seen them plain, the both of them.

"They just never stepped forward. Never tried to stop the coach nor so much as wave their damned shotguns in my direction.

"They just stood there, surrounded by the brush, an' watched me drive past.

"I could've shot them easy. I'm sure they knew that. They were close enough that I could've shot either one of them, maybe both. But they just stood there. An' there ain't no law against standing out in the tullies wearin' linen dusters an' carrying sawed-off scatterguns in their hands. Which is all they done, I tell you.

"They was there. They was all tuned up to rob the stage, but they just stood where they was an' watched me roll past.

"Now why, Charlie? I ask you, why? Why be all ready an' then not say nor do a damn thing but watch me drive past? I don't understand it."

Charlise put an arm around him and said, "It sounds like you could use a drink. You can even light one of those stinking cigars if you like."

Longarm shook his head and scuffed at the floor with a boot then said, "Hold that drink until after dinner. Assuming I'm invited, that is. I need t' go out an' help Will finish with the horses."

Charlie came onto tiptoes and gave him a light kiss on the side of his mouth. "You know you're welcome at my table anytime."

He kissed her back, then put his Stetson on again and headed out the door to join Will, who had taken the coach around behind the building after the passengers left and the mail pouch had been tossed down. Willoughby would pick that up later.

Chapter 48

Longarm skipped supper and went back to the Pickens House and slept alone that night. His mood was simply too foul for him to want company.

The bastards had been there. *Right there!* He saw them. Plain as day. Standing there, shotguns in hand, wearing the linen dusters that were always mentioned in the robbery reports.

The bastards stood there and watched him drive past.

Why?

Why would they do such a thing when they so obviously intended to stop the coach and rob it for the fourth time?

It was a puzzle, and he hated puzzles, at least that kind of puzzle.

In the morning his humor was still bleak. He had a heavy breakfast—there would be no time to indulge himself with lunch while he was driving—and walked over to the Carver Express Company office in darkness to start building the hitch.

"Good morning, Longarm." Will had to repeat the greeting several times before Longarm responded.

"I think I can drive today if you need me," the youngster said.

"Not yet," Longarm told him. "You need t' heal more." He managed a smile. "When we're done with the horses, you can go inside an' help your mother."

"I'm almost healed," Will insisted.

"All right," Longarm said. "Soon as we get 'em hooked up, you can drive the rig around front. See how it feels t' be in the driving box now."

Will nodded eagerly and practically doubled his speed working with the harness and the traces. He climbed onto the tall driver's seat slowly, obviously not quite as agile and ready as he made out to be.

Longarm went inside to greet Charlie and get a cup of coffee while she filled him in on what to expect from the day.

"There's a chance of rain today," she said. "Do you have a slicker?"

"Sure," he told her. "Down in Denver."

"I have one you can use. You really ought to take it."

"I will," he said.

The two of them looked up as Will came in the front. "The passengers and that package are all loaded," he said. "And Longarm . . . you're right. I'm not ready to drive yet."

Will flashed a grin. "Those boys pull hard, don't they. I had forgot."

"Forgotten," Charlie said.

Will's brow furrowed. "Huh?"

"Forgotten. The word is *forgotten*. You said you had forgot. That wasn't right."

"Sorry, Mama. I'll try and remember."

Longarm swallowed down the last of his coffee and pulled his soft leather gloves from his waistband. He grabbed a slicker from a peg beside the door on his way out.

He hoped—almost hoped anyway—that those robbers showed themselves again today.

He knew he was not supposed to, but he would stop the damned coach and go after them on foot if he saw them again. Any passengers could just wait until he got back . . . either with prisoners or with bodies.

Longarm took up the driving lines and made contact with the leaders' bits then popped the whip over their heads.

"Hyah, boys. Hyup."

Chapter 49

"Did you see them again?" Charlie asked when he pulled in that evening.

Longarm shook his head. "Damn them anyway." He handed several packages down to Charlie. She would set them aside for Willoughby to pick up later.

Will came out and took the off leader by the bit to lead him around back for his hay and oats and rubdown. Longarm crawled down off the coach, stiff and aching from the day of handling the four-up.

"Coffee?" Charlie offered, smiling. "I saw you coming. It's hot and waiting for you."

"Thanks." He pulled his gloves off and stuffed them into his waistband then followed her inside.

Charlie stopped in the public part of the office to do some business with two men who wanted tickets for the next day's run. Longarm went on back to the living quarters.

He smiled. She not only had the coffee hot, but had already poured it. And even bought some canned milk and honey to sweeten it.

He sat down at the table and dumped some fixings into his cup.

Whatever Charlie was cooking smelled awfully good. He began looking forward to supper time.

Right now, though, there was work to be done.

He drank his coffee as hot as he could handle it then headed out back to help Will with the horses.

Chapter 50

Longarm awoke to feel Charlise nuzzling the back of his neck.

"Something you want, lady?"

"Yes, there is something I want, mister. And I am no lady."

Longarm rolled over and kissed her, lady or not.

Charlie responded by taking hold of his dick and stroking it awake.

"Now that is more than a mouthful," she mumbled as she kissed her way down his neck, across from nipple to nipple, and down his belly.

"Lovely," she said as she reached the nest of pubic hair at his crotch and the pecker that was sticking tall from it.

Charlie licked her way up one side and down the other before she circled the head with her tongue and finally, exasperatingly, took his cock into her mouth.

Longarm closed his eyes and pressed his head back onto the pillow. He ran his hand over Charlie's hip and between the cheeks of her ass.

"C'mere, woman," he ordered, pulling her on top of him so that they lay head to crotch with each other.

Charlie's pussy tasted faintly salty, although whether that was from her sweat or his residual cum from the previous night, he could not tell. And really did not care.

He found her clit, the little button of her pleasure. It was as firm and erect as his cock was now. He licked it gently. And then not so gently. Until Charlie writhed in pleasure as she came.

She raised herself over him and pressed down until his cock pierced her throat. She gagged a little, then bobbed her head up and down on him.

Longarm felt the gathering of his fluids deep in his balls. Felt the sweet, growing pressure. And the infinitely pleasurable flood of release as he spewed cum into her.

They rolled apart and Charlie fumbled for the cloth she had placed on the nightstand. She handed it to him so he could wipe himself, then took the now wet cloth and used it to cleanse herself.

"Nice," he said.

"Very," Charlie agreed.

They got up and dressed. Longarm started a fire in the stove while Charlie prepared the coffeepot and set it on the stovetop, then began slicing bacon into the pan.

She lifted the towel that covered the biscuit dough she had set out the night before and began spooning dollops of the dough onto a cookie sheet for baking.

It was pleasant in her kitchen, Longarm thought.

And not for the first time, alarm bells rang in his head. Surely he was not tempted by domesticity.

Even so . . .

He went to stand behind Charlie and kissed her while she worked on their breakfast.

Chapter 51

"Is there a Marshal Long here? They said at the Pickens House that he might be here."

"That's me, son. What do you need?"

"I have a telegram for you, Marshal. It came in last night."

Longarm accepted the yellow envelope and gave the boy a nickel. The envelope was not sealed. He sat in the light in Charlie's kitchen to read it, then looked up at her.

"Bad news?" she asked.

"Maybe. It's hard t' say. My boss says these robbers may have moved on someplace else an' I'm wasting my time up here." He smiled. "Billy don't like for his deputies t' waste time. He treats our pay like it was coming out of his own pocket."

"What does that mean then?"

"I have t' go back down home, I reckon," he said.

"I'll miss you," Charlie told him.

"Yeah. Me, too." The thing that surprised him was that he meant it. He had come to enjoy waking up with Charlise Carver warm in the bed beside him. It was one thing to simply fuck a woman; thank you, ma'am, see you later. It was something else entirely to care for her. Longarm had to admit that he was having feelings for Charlie. Fondness, yes, but more than that.

Probably it would be a good thing for him to get back down to Denver for a while. Then he could work out how much he had come to care about her.

"Will can drive today," Charlie said.

"D'you think he's strong enough now? He got beat pretty bad."

"He can do it. We will manage. Don't you worry about us. Go on now. I'll tell Will that he's on the box again." Charlie carefully folded her dish towel and laid it on the table then started out the back door.

"Do you have time to give me a kiss first?" Longarm asked.

She turned and he could see the glitter of tears shining in her eyelashes, but she came into his arms and kissed him long and deep, then jerked away from him and ran out the back door.

Longarm walked into the bedroom to retrieve his coat— he thought that was all he'd left in there—then headed out the front and down the street toward the Pickens House.

He had packing to do and the next possible train to catch.

Chapter 52

Late that afternoon a weary and soot-speckled Custis Long hung his hat on the rack outside Billy Vail's office.

"What d'you need, boss?" he asked the bald United States marshal.

"We have work to do down here, you know. We can't afford to send our deputies on extended vacations in the mountains," Vail reminded.

"It wasn't exactly a vacation," Longarm said, "but I wasn't exactly producing results neither. I get your point. Sorry 'bout that."

"You don't look very sorry," Vail said, "but that is beside the point. I need you down here. We are simply swamped with papers that need to be served, and you are the lad who is being the least productive at your latest assignment. Now see Henry for the paperwork."

Longarm spent the next two days crisscrossing Denver and its suburbs chasing down the recipients of the court documents, most of them summons requests for witnesses, occasionally an arrest warrant.

He put Charlise and Will Carver out of mind and settled

back into the routines of his work as a deputy United States
marshal. He spent his evenings playing low-stakes poker
with friends at one night spot or another, took in a play. And
spent several pleasant hours afterward with an attractive
redhead who appeared in that melodrama.

In short, he was at home, his fling in Fairplay nearly
forgotten.

On Thursday he took time out to get a haircut and have
his boots shined by a smiling kid whose age he guessed
at ten or eleven. He chatted with the barber for a few minutes and read the morning newspaper while he was in the
chair.

Afterward, smelling of Pinaud Clubman and feeling
plenty chipper, he strolled the long way around to get back
to the office.

All that waited for him there, he was sure, were more
warrants, more summonses, more paperwork. Paperwork
was not Longarm's favorite. He much preferred being out
in the field where the criminals were.

He stopped in at a tobacconist's shop and treated himself
to a Hernandez y Hernandez panatela along with a box of
fresh cheroots. Stopped at a haberdashery and admired—but
did not buy—the dress shirts on sale there. Paused at a boot-
maker's and priced—but did not buy—a new pair of custom
boots.

Finally, unable to avoid the inevitable, he returned to the
office.

"Where have you been?" Henry, Billy Vail's clerk,
demanded when he walked in. "The boss has been howling
for you for the past half hour."

"What's up?" Longarm asked, hanging his Stetson on
the hat tree.

"Up in Park County. There's been another of those mail

robberies, and the district postmaster is yelling even louder than the marshal."

"Just give me time t' grab my bag, an' I'll be on the next train up," Longarm said, retrieving the hat he had just relinquished.

Chapter 53

He caught the same up-bound train and again reached Fairplay in the middle of the night. Instead of checking into the Pickens House this time, he walked past it, went around to the back of the Carver Express Company, and knocked on Charlise's door.

When she came to see who was there at such an hour, Longarm cheerfully announced, "There's a weary traveler out here in search o' rest. An' maybe something else, too."

Charlie laughed and unlocked her door. "Custis. I was hoping they would send you again. I take it you heard what happened?"

"No details," he said. "Just that it did happen. D'you happen t' have any coffee left over? An' let me look at you, girl. You're a sight for sore eyes."

Charlie was wearing a slightly tattered terry cloth robe and her hair was a bird's nest. Longarm smiled to himself. She had not let him see the old robe before, and she had always been careful to keep her hair brushed when he was around. This evening he took her by surprise and saw her without any efforts to doll up. It was rather flattering, he thought, that she had been so careful about those things before.

"You look terrific," he said, lying only a very little. He took Charlie into his arms, lifted her chin, and gave her a long, lingering kiss.

Charlie's tongue probed into his mouth and her left hand sought out the bulge behind his fly.

"I'm glad you are here," she whispered, holding him tight. "Are you tired after the trip up?"

"Mm-hmm," he mumbled.

"Come to bed. We'll talk in the morning."

"Fine, but is Will all right? I wasn't given any details," he asked, pulling away from the kiss but keeping an arm around Charlie's waist.

"He's fine. Angry. I think a little frightened although he wouldn't admit to it."

"He should be. When people with guns stop an' rob you, you got every right t' be scared," Longarm said.

"Really, Custis. We can talk about all of that in the morning." She smiled and tugged him forward. "Come to bed now. I want to feel you inside me again."

Charlie giggled. "Just those few days and I was missing that beautiful cock of yours."

"Then let's us do somethin' about that, darlin'," Longarm said, allowing himself to be dragged into the tiny bedroom.

Chapter 54

"Good Lord, Custis!" Charlie sat up and wiped her lips with the back of her hand. "You were only away for a couple days, and you built up that much cum? I thought you were going to drown me."

He laughed and pulled her down beside him. When he kissed her, she tasted salty and warm from his cum.

Longarm fondled Charlie's right tit and toyed with the nipple.

"That feels *so* good," she mumbled. "Can you get it up again?"

"Can a goose honk?" he said.

Charlie gave him a playful slap on the chest. "That isn't an answer, silly."

"Hell, I kinda thought it was."

Charlie laughed and once again bent over Longarm, taking him into the warmth of her mouth. He quickly grew and strengthened, his cock returning to its previous state of eagerness.

"Impressive," Charlie said, sitting upright. "But what can it *do*?"

"Let me show you what it can do," Longarm told her. He took her by the shoulder and pulled her down onto her back, slid a hand between her legs, and pried them apart then rolled on top of her.

Charlie reached down between her legs and took hold of him. With her help, his cock found the way home, sliding into her. Filling her. Bumping up against the little, peach-shaped bulb deep inside her.

"Did I hurt you?"

"What? I'm not supposed to move?"

Both of them laughed.

This is good, Longarm thought. This is the way it's supposed to be between a man and a woman who like each other. That's the key ingredient: That they *like* each other.

It occurred to him that, yes, he very much liked Charlise Carver.

"What's your maiden name?" he asked mid-stroke.

"Where did that come from?" she shot back at him.

"I dunno. I just wondered, that's all."

"You pick a fine time to ask things like that."

"You don't have t' answer if you don't want to."

"Charlise Elizabeth Randolph Carver, Randolph being my name before I got married. Satisfied?"

"Yeah. Thanks." He chuckled and nibbled on her ear, pulled back, and drove forward, harder now and faster until he came once again, this time spitting not quite so much cum into her after she so efficiently swallowed his first heavy load.

He quivered, driving deep inside her, and Charlie clasped him and shuddered in her own sweet spasm of release.

It was good to be back, he thought.

Chapter 55

"You're back," Will exclaimed the next morning when he walked in and saw Longarm seated at the table with a cup of coffee.

"Obviously," Longarm said. "We heard there was another robbery, so the bastards haven't moved on. Sit down, Will. Tell me about it."

Will glanced first at his mother, then pulled out the chair Longarm indicated and sat. Charlie poured a cup of coffee for her son then turned back to the stove, where she was working on a skillet of very aromatic bacon.

"There isn't much to tell," Will said. "It was the same as before. They stepped out of the brush, all covered with their dusters and flour sack masks, one on each side of the road, carrying those ugly damn sawed-off shotguns.

"They never said a word, either one of them, just gestured with the guns. That was enough. I pulled to a stop and tossed the mail down to them, and they backed away. I waited until they were back in the brush alongside the road and started off again.

"The funny thing was, this trip I was carrying a strongbox. I don't know what was in it. Not for sure. But it was sent from a mine in Bailey to a bank down in Colorado City. So I assume it was raw gold though, like I say, I never actually saw what was in there.

"Surely whatever was in that strongbox was a lot more than could have been in the five letters I was carrying at the time. But all the robbers took was the letters.

"Maybe they didn't know about the gold. I have to believe that they didn't. But they could have robbed me of that, too." Will shook his head, leaned forward, and blew on the coffee. He took his coffee black, just like his mother.

"Were there any passengers?" Longarm asked.

"One. The robbers never tried to take anything from him."

"This passenger," Longarm said. "Is he a regular on your runs? I mean, could he be signaling the robbers somehow?"

"I never saw the man before," Will said, "and if he was giving them any sort of signal, I certainly never saw him do it. They ignored him. All they took was the mail, and there was precious little of that on that day."

Longarm grunted, deep in thought, and sipped at his coffee.

He paid attention, though, when Charlie set plates of bacon, biscuits, and red-eye gravy in front of them.

When it came time to go out to the coach, Longarm said, "I'll ride with you t'day. An' this time I brought my rifle along. If we see the sons o' bitches lurking along the road, I can reach out to 'em with it whether they want to step forward an' challenge us or not."

"In that case," Will said, "I hope to hell the bastards try to rob us today."

"We'll give them the opportunity," Longarm said. "That seems to be the best we can do. The rest is up to them." He wiped his lips with the napkin, stood, and gave Charlie a kiss. If Will objected to Longarm's show of affection for his mother, he did not show it.

Chapter 56

For three days Longarm rode "shotgun" on Will Carver's stagecoach. He did not so much as catch a glimpse of the hooded pair in the linen dusters that he had seen once before.

Saturday evening he helped Will rub down the horses, check their hooves, and clean the harness. Longarm was up to his elbows in neat's-foot oil when Charlie came out back.

"You have a visitor, Custis," she said, then added, "and supper will be ready in fifteen minutes."

"All right, thanks." He laid aside the oily rag he had been using on the harness and rolled his sleeves down. He used a dry rag to wipe his hands then buttoned his sleeves and picked up his coat, putting it on as he headed for the back door and on through to the office.

"Willboughby," he said, greeting the Fairplay postmaster. "What brings you here on a Saturday night? I would have thought you'd be out carousing."

Longarm's humor passed completely over the head of the small, clerkish postmaster. If there was anyone in Fairplay less likely to be carousing on a Saturday night, Longarm had not met the man.

"I want to talk to you, Long," Willoughby said.

"Sure. What about?"

"Could we sit down," the little man said.

"O' course, but let's go outside an' set on the porch. I'd like to smoke an' Mrs. Carver don't like the smell of it." He motioned Willoughby ahead and followed the little man, already reaching in his coat for a cheroot.

Once settled into rocking chairs on the front porch, Longarm flicked a match aflame and lit his cheroot. "What's on your mind?"

"I want to know how close you are to capturing the brigands who have been robbing the mails," Willoughby said.

"Hell, I don't know what t' tell you. I been riding with the coach an' carrying a rifle, but so far they haven't showed themselves."

"In other words, you have not been accomplishing anything," Willoughby said.

"You could put it that way, but what else do you think I should do?" Longarm told him.

"The reason I ask," Willoughby said, "is that I have been in contact with the postmaster general. He is asking for my recommendation as to whether the mail contract with Carver Express Company should be terminated and someone else given the job. In fact, he is asking who I would suggest take over the mail route."

Longarm puffed on his cheroot in silence for a moment while he digested the meaning of what Willoughby had just said.

If the mail contract was revoked, he knew, it would ruin Charlise and Will. The company could not survive without the income provided by the post office. The Carver Express Company would go into bankruptcy, and Charlie would be without the future she was trying to provide for herself and her son.

It was a harsh prospect, he thought.

"Can you hold off with that recommendation?" he asked.

"For a few days, I suppose. Do you think you can catch them?"

"T' tell you the truth, Jon, I don't know. But give me a few days t' stew on this, will you?"

"A few days then," Willoughby said, standing and brushing the seat of his trousers. "I'll write back to the postmaster general and tell him I need more time to come up with my recommendation."

Longarm nodded. "All right. Thanks. I'll, uh, I'll let you know if I think of anything. An' you'll be the first t' know if I catch the sons o' bitches."

"Good night then, Marshal." Willoughby turned and hurried away down the street toward the business district.

Longarm stayed where he was, smoking and pondering, until Charlie came out to call him in for supper.

Chapter 57

Longarm and Charlie spent Sunday in bed except for getting up to eat and to tend to the horses. Their small talk was mostly about the robbers. Longarm had not told her what Willoughby said about the postmaster general and the possibility that she could lose the mail contract.

That was the subject that preyed on his mind the whole day, however.

Several times Charlie asked what he was so deep in thought about.

"Oh, nothing," he responded each time, adding a smile to his lies.

"If you say so." She obviously knew that he was lying, but she did not challenge him any further.

Will seemed to accept coming to meals and seeing his mother wearing nothing but a bathrobe. It was obvious that she was barefoot and happy at her stove.

After supper Will invited Longarm to go into town for a drink.

"My treat," he said.

"Sounds fine. Let me get my coat an' hat."

When they were out on the street, Will said. "Would you have any problem going down to Maybelle's for that drink, Custis?"

"No, o' course not," Longarm said, lengthening his stride and heading in that direction.

Maybelle's whorehouse was busy when they got there, typical for a day when the miners and most businessmen were off work and had both free time and a little money to spend.

Will led the way into the parlor. A cute little redhead attached herself to Will and told Longarm, "Ma'am says you should get first pick of any of the girls and never mind who's in line ahead of you. I guess you're something special, huh?"

"Not really. An' I just came in here t' have a drink with Will. I won't be needin' a girl tonight so there's no cause t' get folks upset about who's next in line."

He looked across the room to where Maybelle was standing at the wide doorway and gave the madam a salute with a forefinger to the brim of his Stetson.

Maybelle smiled and turned away to tend to business elsewhere.

"What are you drinking, Marshal?" a young Hispanic woman asked.

"Rye whiskey," he said. "Neat."

"Yes sir." She was gone only a minute or so before she returned with a tumbler of excellent rye for Longarm and a tall, fruity something for Will. Will paid for both drinks.

Over the rim of his glass Will said, "You know, don't you, that my mom is hoping you'll stay up here permanently."

"You mean buy into the line?" Longarm asked.

"Or into her," Will said.

"I didn't know . . . look, Will, I got a job already. It's a good job an' I like to think I'm pretty good at it. But except for carrying this badge, I'm not really a very permanent kind o' fellow. I mean . . . I like your mother a lot an' I know she likes me, but . . . I'm not gonna marry her an' I don't figure to buy into the stage line neither. I hope you understand that. More important, I hope she'll understand it."

Will nodded. "Good," he said and took a drink of whatever it was he had ordered.

"You're all right with that?" Longarm asked.

"Truth is, I prefer it," Will said. "Mama deserves to be happy, and I hope she is, but I have the feeling that you are not the man she needs. Not in the long run, that is. Uh, no offense intended."

"None taken," Longarm said.

"Good," Will said again. He drained his glass and stood, heading for the little redhead who had greeted them when they arrived.

Longarm took his time with his rye then stood and ambled over to the doorway.

"Thanks for your courtesy," he told Maybelle on his way out.

Chapter 58

Longarm lay awake that night after Charlise had gone to sleep. He listened to her soft breathing, felt the warmth of her naked body next to his. She was a nice woman, pleasant and sincere. She deserved a good man. A man better than he was, he thought.

His conversation with Will got him to thinking. About Charlise and the Carver Express Company but also about the recurrent mail robberies that threatened to take away their mail contract and drive them into bankruptcy.

The robberies made little sense, he thought. To take a few pieces of mail and leave the strongbox certainly made no sense whatsoever.

Except it did. To someone, to those two robbers, it made perfect sense.

If only Longarm knew or could figure out what that was.

He lay awake long into the night and in the morning over breakfast with Charlie and Will announced, "I'm headin' back down to Denver today. Obviously I'm wasting my time an' the government's money being up here and ridin' shotgun guard atop your coach.

"My guess is that they keep a watch, an' if they see me coming, they just don't show themselves. I figure they believe they're in enough trouble with the U.S. government by robbin' from the mail. They don't wanta compound it by shooting a deputy U.S. marshal, too. So if they see me, they just lay low an' let the coach roll on by.

"Point is, I could ride up there forever an' not do you or the government any good. So I'm goin' on back to Denver. I'm sorry 'bout this, Charlie, but it's what I think best. Soon as we get those big boys hitched an' Will has 'em rolling, I'll walk over to the depot and see to the next train down."

Will gave Longarm a long look. Then he nodded and silently mouthed, "Thank you."

Charlie began to cry. When her sobbing became obvious, she jumped up from the table and ran into the bedroom, slamming the door shut behind her.

Longarm sighed, long and deep. He hated the thought that he made the woman cry like that. He hurt her with that announcement, but it was the right thing to do.

"Come on, Will," he said, rising from the table. "I'll help you get that hitch put together."

Chapter 59

Longarm stepped off the train in Denver just after 5 p.m. He went outside and hailed the first cab waiting in line there.

"Where to, mister?" the cabbie asked as Longarm climbed into his vehicle.

"Federal Building, an' make it as quick as you can."

"At this time of day, mister, all those offices will be closed before I can get you there," the hack driver called down from his box.

"Not the one I need," Longarm said. "Just do it, please, without argument."

"Whatever you say, mister." The hack was in motion before Longarm had time to sit down.

The driver pulled his rig to a halt on the side of Colfax Avenue at five forty-two according to Longarm's railroad grade pocket watch. He nodded, satisfied, and gave the man a generous tip on top of his fare.

Longarm carried his bag up the steps fronting Colfax and tried the door. It was open. So was the U.S. Marshal's Office.

As he had expected, Henry was at his desk cleaning up the day's paperwork.

"Is the boss in?" Longarm asked.

If Henry was surprised to see Longarm there, he did not show it. "He's in," was all he said.

"I'd like t' see him," Longarm said.

Henry nodded, stood, and took a moment to stretch, then went to Billy Vail's door and knocked softly. A moment later they heard Billy's "Come in."

Henry entered and returned only moments later. "Go on in," he said.

"You got them?" Billy asked when Longarm stepped into his office.

"Not yet," Longarm said. "But I got an idea how we can smoke 'em out. It's just that I need your help, boss. And, uh, maybe get you t' pull some strings on the political side o' things."

"Sit down," Vail said. "Tell me what's on your mind here."

"Yes, sir," Longarm said, pulling a chair around and dropping into it. "Now what I'm thinkin' . . ."

Five minutes later Vail leaned back in his chair and steepled his hands beneath his chin while he thought about Longarm's plan. He pondered the request only briefly. Then he nodded. "In the morning," Billy said. "We'll get to work on this in the morning."

Chapter 60

Again it was late at night when the up-bound freight dropped Longarm at the Fairplay depot. This time he dragged his battered and much-traveled carpetbag to the Pickens House.

"Marshal Long. How nice to see you again, sir," the clerk said, wide awake and cheerful despite the hour.

"Evenin', Nathan. D'you have a room for me?" Longarm said.

"You know we'll always provide for your needs, Marshal." Nathan grinned. "Even if I have to kick someone else out. Which, fortunately, I do not." Nathan turned and plucked a key off the board behind his desk and said, "You can have number eight again if that is all right."

"Fine."

Nathan raised his voice and called, "Johnny. Wake up, lad. Time to work."

Longarm smiled. "There's no need t' bother the boy, Nathan. I know where the room is, an' I can handle this bag by myself until I get up there."

"Even so," Nathan said, "it is our policy and our pleasure

to serve you. Besides, you need some water if you want to wash off the soot and cinders from traveling."

"Thank you," Longarm said.

"Johnny!"

The boy came stumbling out of the back room, rubbing his eyes and trying to wake up.

"Take Marshal Long's bag up to eight," Nathan said, "and bring him some water once you get him settled."

"Yes, sir. Do you want the tub, sir?"

"A pitcher will do for tonight," Longarm said.

"Yes, sir." Johnny reached for Longarm's bag and started up the stairs, Longarm following.

Longarm waited until the boy brought his water, then tipped the kid and bolted the door.

He stripped and washed himself then crawled into bed, tired but satisfied.

In the morning, Charlise Carver got the devastating news that her mail contract was canceled as of the end of the month.

She spent the day huddled in her room crying. Will went on a bender that ended with him being thrown in jail on a charge of drunk and disorderly.

It was not the best of days for the Carvers.

Chapter 61

"You can't possibly understand, Custis," Charlie said that evening, sobbing lightly but no longer blubbering the way she had been most of the day. "It isn't your livelihood that has been lost. It isn't your future that is ruined."

"You still have the coach line," Longarm reasoned. "You still have your passenger business."

"You've seen how few passengers we carry," Charlie said. "The stagecoach business is just an accommodation for the people up here in South Park. We make our living from the mail contract. Without that income, we will go under inside a month, two at the most."

"Want some unsolicited advice?" he asked.

"Certainly. Any suggestions would be welcome right now," Charlie said.

"I been watching you an' your outfit," Longarm said, "an' I'm sure you can increase your profit if you get rid o' this heavy Concord coach. It takes the four-up to pull it. Replace it with a light mud wagon. As little passenger trade as you get, a retired army ambulance would do everything you need done an' with half the horses to feed.

"Pull it with a pair instead o' a four-up and you've cut your expenses in half right there.

"You can get mud wagons cheap down in Manitou or Colorado City. Likely sell the Concord down there, too, since they get a lot o' passenger traffic running from one town to another.

"I'd think the light wagon would have an easier time in winter, too. The Concord has t' be dragged through the snow. A mud wagon, you could put runners on instead of wheels and use it as a sled. Easiest thing possible. Will would know how."

"Do you really think we could make a go of it?" Charlie asked.

"It's certainly worth a try. Cut your expenses in half, you just might could do it," Longarm said.

"I don't know."

"Try it, lady. Lord knows you won't get anywhere by laying down an' letting life walk on you."

Charlie lifted her chin and tried to smile. She did not quite make it, but it was a beginning. "Come in to dinner, Custis. Will should be home with the coach soon."

"I'd be pleased to," Longarm said, leaning down and kissing her lightly on the corner of her mouth. She would not be in any mood for screwing tonight, he was sure, but he could offer comfort that did not involve anything serious.

And he wanted to offer comfort. Just not . . . too much.

Chapter 62

Longarm slept with Charlise that night but spooned next to her without passion or sex, wanting to offer comfort instead of a hard dick.

In the morning he very gently made love to her again, lying behind her and coming into her while they lay on their sides. He stroked in and out slowly and quietly, allowing her to climax before him and only then speeding up enough to reach his own long, sweet release.

When he was done, Charlie turned over in his arms to face him. "Thank you, Custis. That was nice."

"My pleasure, ma'am," he said, the corners of his eyes crinkling, "an' I mean that sincerely."

"We should get up now," Charlie said, kissing him.

"Mm-hm."

"No, I mean it."

"I'm not arguing," he said.

"No, but you are blocking the way. You need to move so I can get out of the bed."

"Oops. Sorry." He swung his legs off the bed and sat up, his hair tousled and even his mustache bristly.

Charlie grabbed a robe and went into the kitchen to build up the fire and get the coffee started. Longarm stood, yawning and stretching, and wobbled over to the bureau to pour some water into the basin and wash.

He felt his chin. He could use a shave, but that could wait.

"How long before breakfast?" he asked when he emerged, dressed, into the kitchen.

"Give me a half hour. Will should be here then. We can talk about your ideas."

"My ideas?"

"The mud wagon and the two-horse hitch," she said. "I like that. We can sell the surplus horses and the big coach. That will help. I don't know why . . . well, I suppose I do know why I've been doing things this way."

Longarm's eyebrows went up in inquiry.

"I have been doing it this way," Charlie said, "because Hank Blaisdell did it this way. Of course, when he owned the line, there was much more passenger traffic. That was before the railroad came in, and the routes shrank down to what we have now. But Hank already had his big coach and the heavy horses, and I just took over from him and continued on doing things the way Hank had done. That made sense before the railroad. Not so much now, as you so gently pointed out."

Longarm bent down to kiss her, then reached for his coat.

"Are you going somewhere?" she asked.

"I have an errand t' run. I won't be but a couple minutes." He smiled and said, "I'll be back by the time the coffee is done."

Longarm stepped out into the chill of the predawn and set off at a brisk pace, but true to his word, he was back within minutes.

Charlie smiled when he came in. "Just in time," she said.

"See. I tol' you so." He sat at the table, and Charlie set a cup of steaming coffee—and the condiments to go with it—before him.

Will joined them a few minutes later, just in time for a hearty breakfast of flapjacks and pork chops.

"Will you be riding with me today, Marshal?" Will asked.

Longarm nodded and reached for the syrup. "Aye, I will if you don't mind."

"All right then." Will flashed a smile. "In that case, you can help me get the boys in harness and hitched up."

It occurred to Longarm that Will would miss his four-ups if Charlie did choose to make the changes he had suggested. The young man liked each and every one of his animals and might regret having to cut their livestock—even if that meant cutting their expenses—by half.

"Whenever you're ready," Longarm said, dropping his napkin beside his plate and standing.

Chapter 63

For the next four days, Sunday included, the first thing Long-arm did each morning after getting dressed was to walk over to the railroad depot on his unspecified "errands."

On Monday morning he returned to the Carver Express Company office with a smile. "Good news," he said.

"I could certainly use some of that," Charlie told him.

"I sent a wire to a friend of mine down in Denver. He runs a livery out by the stockyards. I asked him to keep an eye peeled for a mud wagon. He says he's found the perfect outfit for you. It's a delivery wagon. Used to belong to a greengrocer. Closed body but lightweight. Just add some benches and you're in business. It's light enough for one horse to pull but it can be set up for a pair. How does that sound?"

"Expensive," Charlie said.

"Twenty-five dollars," Longarm returned.

"Twenty-five? That's all? Tell him I'll take it."

Longarm grinned. "I already did. He'll send it up on the late freight this afternoon. Soon as we get it ready, with your name painted on it an' everything, you can send the Concord down an' he'll sell it for you. I'd say you should get a hundred dollars, maybe a hundred twenty-five, for it."

"Oh, Custis, that is wonderful." Charlie threw her arms around his neck and was in the process of giving him a very appreciative kiss—and promising considerably more than that—when Will came in for his breakfast.

"If you two want to be alone, I can leave and get something to eat at the café," Will said.

"No need," Longarm said. "We're just practicing."

"Honey, wait until I tell you the news," Charlie said.

"From the sound of your voice, it must be good news," Will said.

"Oh, it is, honey. It really is."

Charlie informed Will of their good fortune, and he whistled appreciatively. "Wow. I think . . . I know which horses I want to keep. The sturdiest. And the youngest that are steady. The rest we can send down to be sold. Or find a buyer up here maybe." He smiled. "This will work out fine in winter. The snow can get pretty deep between Bailey and Lake George. Not so much from Guffey up to Hartsel."

Will looked at Longarm. "You say we can put sled runners on the wagon?"

"Easy," Longarm said.

"They won't be needed much of the time, but there are days when runners would come in handy." Will looked at his mother and said, "We just might make a go of it, even without the mail contract."

"You can thank Custis if we do," Charlise said.

"I will, but I think I'll just offer to buy him a drink instead of kissing him like that."

"The drink I will accept," Longarm said. "But no kiss, thank you."

"Seriously, this is great news," Will said. "The best we've had since the mail contract was canceled."

"Good. That's what I was hoping for," Longarm told him. "Now let's eat up some of your mama's good cooking an' get to work. Those horses won't put their own harnesses on, y'know."

Chapter 64

On Tuesday he returned from the depot with an envelope in hand. He gave Charlie the obligatory morning kiss and accepted the cup of coffee she handed him—already fixed with condensed milk and two spoons of sugar—then asked, "Who is Grant Godfrey?"

Charlie gave him a quizzical look. "Whatever brought that layabout to mind, Custis?"

"You know him then?"

"Yes, of course. Godfrey is Jon Willoughby's brother-in-law. He lives with Jon and Erma." She rolled her eyes. "I don't think that man has done a day's work since he came up here. Rumor has it that he was in prison for a spell, but I don't know that for sure. He could get work if he wanted it. The mines are practically begging for workers. But not Godfrey. He would rather cadge drinks at the Iron Horse Tavern. And I apologize. I shouldn't go on like that. I hardly know the man."

Will walked in and Charlie said, "Sit down. I'll have breakfast on the table in a minute or two. Have some coffee while you wait. Do you need a refill yet, Custis? No?"

Charlie poured coffee for her son and turned back to her stove.

"Interesting thing about Godfrey," Longarm said.

"It is? What in the world could be interesting about him? And why did his name come up anyway?" Charlie asked, her back to the two of them.

Longarm chuckled and leaned back in his chair. "The reason I ask is because Jonathan Willoughby is highly recommending that Grant Godfrey be awarded the mail contract to serve the South Park area."

"How would you know?"

He smiled. "This whole thing has been a setup. I talked to my boss down in Denver 'bout how we might be able to smoke out the bandits. It occurred to me one night that the robbers were only interested in taking the mail. It didn't have any value, but that's what they wanted.

"So I got to wonderin' why they would do such a thing. They robbed the mail and somebody seemed t' be trying to stop Will from driving an' carrying that mail. One way or another, they were tryin' to stop it.

"An' what was valuable? It was the mail contract itself that was valuable. Regular money sent by the Fed'ral government each an' every month. You were getting it. Somebody else wanted it.

"So my boss got together with the postmaster general an' had him post, nice an' official, that your mail contract was bein' terminated. Which it isn't, by the way. Your contract is still valid an' will go on just like always. The cancellation was a ruse to see who wanted to take it over.

"Now we know. Grant Godfrey and Jon Willoughby would seem to be the bastards that tried to ruin you, Charlise, tried t' ruin you and the Carver Express Company.

"I'm betting it was them doing the holdups for just exactly that purpose. An' they figured since Willoughby already had the post office up here, he could slide his brother-in-law into the mail route award. The family would have that much more money each month. They didn't want the trouble an' the expense of the stagecoach line. Just the mail, an' no more than what passes through here, they could handle that from the back of a horse real easy.

"I already knew something was up because last Friday, Beaver Jones mentioned something about some fella coming by, wanting t' keep a spare horse where you keep your relay team. Now we know who that woulda been. An' why."

"What will you do now?" Charlie asked, hurrying to flip her griddle of hotcakes quick before they burned.

Longarm smiled. "I got handcuffs for the both of 'em," he said. "Now put some o' those cakes on my plate an' hand me the sorghum, if you please."

Watch for

**LONGARM AND THE ROCK SPRINGS
RECKONING**

the 434th novel in the exciting LONGARM
series from Jove

Coming in January!